"If it comes to selling, if it's what you have to do, I'll buy the place myself."

She laughed. "Yeah, right."

Nathan cleared his throat and looked up, not wanting to sound arrogant but needing her to know it wasn't an empty offer. That he could buy it tomorrow and come up with the cash immediately if he had to. "I'm serious."

Her laughter died, the uneasy smile wiped from her face. She studied him, eyes no longer full of tears—her gaze was serious now. "You could actually buy this place, just like that?" she asked.

He shrugged, not wanting to make a big deal out of it. A year ago, hell, a few months ago, he'd have had no problem letting anyone know what he could afford, but since coming here...he just didn't want to be that guy anymore. Staying on the farm had given him the break he'd needed, and it had also given him a fresh start, even if he was going to have to face reality and head home one day soon.

"Yeah, I could. But if I did I'd need a manager, so there's no chance I'd evict you."

Jessica smiled, but he knew she wasn't sure what to say or how to take his words.

Dear Reader

We often take the country in which we live for granted, but I'm proud to say that I never feel that way about New Zealand. It's a very special place, and I'm fortunate to live on a small farm that is also home to our four horses. This made writing THE BILLIONAIRE IN DISGUISE all the more special, because I was able to set the story on a beautiful horse ranch in the north island of my home country.

When I first started thinking about Nathan Bell, the troubled yet handsome hero in this book, I wanted the story to take place somewhere he could visit to relax and recover. So I created the ranch that was home to heroine Jessica Falls, where they could horseback-ride, enjoy one another's company, and ultimately heal. Personally, this is exactly the kind of location I love!

Nathan and Jessica have both experienced terrible loss, which draws them together and pushes them apart. From rural New Zealand to bustling London, their journey to love spans two countries before they finally find their happy-ever-after.

Soraya

THE BILLIONAIRE IN DISGUISE

BY
SORAYA LANE

Published in Great Britain 2014
by Mills & Boon, an imprint of Harlequin (UK) Limited,
Eton House, 18-24 Paradise Road, Richmond, Surrey, TW9 1SR

© 2014 Soraya Lane

ISBN: 978-0-263-24316-1

Harlequin (UK) Limited's policy is to use papers that are natural,
renewable and recyclable products and made from wood grown in
sustainable forests. The logging and manufacturing processes conform
to the legal environmental regulations of the country of origin.

Printed and bound in Great Britain
by CPI Antony Rowe, Chippenham, Wiltshire

Writing for Mills & Boon® is truly a dream come true for **Soraya Lane**. An avid book-reader and writer since her childhood, Soraya describes becoming a published author as 'the best job in the world', and hopes to be writing heart-warming, emotional romances for many years to come.

Soraya lives with her own real-life hero on a small farm in New Zealand, surrounded by animals and with an office overlooking a field where their horses graze.

For more information about Soraya and her upcoming releases visit her at her website, www.sorayalane.com, her blog, www.sorayalane.blogspot.com, or follow her at www.facebook.com/SorayaLaneAuthor

Recent books by Soraya Lane:

HER SOLDIER PROTECTOR**
THE RETURNING HERO**
PATCHWORK FAMILY IN THE OUTBACK*
MISSION: SOLDIER TO DADDY
THE SOLDIER'S SWEETHEART
THE NAVY SEAL'S BRIDE
BACK IN THE SOLDIER'S ARMS
RODEO DADDY
THE ARMY RANGER'S RETURN
SOLDIER ON HER DOORSTEP

Bellaroo Creek!
**The Soldiers' Homecoming*

**This and other titles by Soraya Lane
are available in eBook format
from www.millsandboon.co.uk**

DEDICATION

I am so fortunate to have an amazing support network,
and that includes some very special author friends.
From daily email chats, text messages and
writing sprints, it all means so much to me.
Thank you Natalie Anderson, Nicola Marsh,
Yvonne Lindsay and Tessa Radley, for
your constant encouragement, support and friendship.

CHAPTER ONE

JESSICA FALLS LEANED against the wooden fence and stared out at the land. She hadn't been home in almost two years, but there was nothing about her surroundings that wasn't familiar to her. The horses grazing in the fields, the smell of the pine trees, the big house behind her—they were all things ingrained in her memory that she would never forget, no matter how long she lived.

But nothing was like it used to be. She wiped away tears that had escaped from the corner of her eye, despite her best efforts to blink them away, and forced herself to turn and go back to the house. She'd only just arrived back, but instead of going straight in she'd walked around outside and done her best to ignore reality. *That she wasn't going to have to live in the house alone, that her grandfather wasn't really gone, that she hadn't just lost everything that mattered to her.*

Jessica moved slowly up the veranda steps, stopping when she reached the door and taking a deep breath. She eventually put her key in the lock and pushed the door open, listening to it creak as she stared into the dark hallway. She picked up one of her suitcases and wheeled it in behind her, moving slowly to the bottom of the stairs. It was quiet, too silent for her liking, but it was something she was going to have to get used to.

"Hello?"

She jumped and turned at the sound of a deep voice, not expecting anyone else to be on the property, let alone at her front door.

"Sorry, I didn't mean to startle you."

Jessica locked eyes with a man leaning against her doorjamb. Who the hell was he? She slipped her hand into her back pocket, feeling for her phone, ready to dial for help if she needed it.

"Ah, can I help you?" She didn't care how handsome the guy was—she didn't want company right now, and definitely not from some stranger.

"I saw you arrive before and I wanted to say hi."

Jessica stood still for a moment, silent, before she realized who he was and felt like a complete idiot. She prized her fingers from her phone and pushed her hands into her pockets instead.

"You're the guy renting the cottage, right?" she asked, wishing she hadn't glared at him like he was some kind of intruder. Her granddad's lawyer had told her all about the guest staying on the grounds, and she'd forgotten about him. "The jet lag must be getting to me."

His smile was genuine when he flashed it, his eyes crinkling ever so at the corners to match the upturn of his mouth.

"Understandable. I only knew Jock a couple of months and I'm already missing him like hell, so I can't imagine how you're feeling right now."

Jessica sighed, not ready to talk about it. She'd just traveled all the way from London without sleeping a wink, left her best horse behind without knowing if she'd ever be able to afford to bring him home, and everything was fast catching up on her. Not to mention the fact that she'd missed the funeral service of the one person in the world she really cared about, because she'd been stuck in a hospital on the other side of the world. Her granddad had been her only family since her mom had died, and she couldn't shake the feeling that she was an orphan now. And the fact she hadn't had the chance to say goodbye to him.

"Is there anything I can do for you? I'm not really sure what your arrangement was with my granddad, but you're welcome to stay for as long as you want."

It wasn't that she particularly wanted anyone hanging around, but from the information she'd received to date, she was going to need the income from the cottage just to keep paying the bills. And from what she'd heard, this guy was paying a small fortune in rent. He wasn't exactly hard to look at, either—brown eyes flecked with gold, dark hair that was a little too long and a smile that made her want to stare at his mouth way longer than she should have.

"I won't get in your way, I just wanted to say hi," he told her. "I'm Nathan."

"Jessica," she replied, holding out her hand and

pressing her palm to his. "But I'm guessing you already knew that."

"Not a day went past that Jock didn't talk about you, so yeah." He pushed his hands into his jean pockets and took a step backward. "I'll see you around, Jessica. Take care."

Jessica smiled and raised one hand in a half wave, wishing he hadn't just surprised her so soon after arriving. Any other day she'd have been better prepared, would have remembered her manners and invited him in for a coffee just like her grandfather would have, but today was tough. Today was about coming to terms with losing everything. Tomorrow she'd try to start rebuilding, and figure out how the hell she was going to save the only place that had ever been home to her. Trouble was, she was used to being a loner, so it was weird having someone she didn't know staying on the property.

She watched him go, the casual way he sauntered off toward the stables, hands still thrust in his pockets, as if he didn't have a worry in the world. Everything felt like it was crashing around her, but she had to stay strong, needed to hold herself together, because that was what her granddad would have expected, and she didn't want to let him down.

Nathan Bell gave the horse a pat and dropped to the ground, nudging his hat down lower over his head, crossing his ankles and shutting his eyes. The sun was warm but not too hot, and he was feeling lazy as hell. He knew Patch wouldn't walk off on him, and he just needed to try to catch up on some sleep. Since Jock had died, his insomnia had come back, and right now he was beat.

He was always worse at night, the memories of finding his wife, the weight of what had happened, always seeking him out in the dark. During the day, he usually managed to keep them at bay, but forgetting what had happened was impossible.

He'd just drifted off, was falling into the sleep he'd been craving, when he received a sharp kick in the leg.

"Ouch!"

"What the hell do you think you're doing?"

Nathan pushed his hat up and found himself staring straight up at Jessica. What the hell was *he* doing? What the hell was *she* doing? Her eyes looked wild, face mad as hell. At least it took his mind off his nightmares.

"I was sleeping, but I'm guessing you already figured that out," he said, drawing one of his legs up and rubbing the spot where she'd kicked him. He had no idea what he'd done to make her so angry between now and when he'd met her.

"I mean what the hell are you doing here? And with my granddad's horse?"

She was seriously pissed with him, that much was obvious, and he doubted he was going to get back to sleep anytime soon. Nathan tried not to smile—she'd looked pretty when he'd met her at the house, even with her tearstained cheeks, but she was gorgeous as sin all fired up and angry.

"Jock used to bring me here, as soon as he'd taught me to ride," Nathan told her, wishing she'd back a step up instead of standing over him and glaring like he'd just stolen something from her. "And the last few weeks before he passed away he wasn't up to riding, so he asked me to take Patch out for him."

"I don't believe you." Her tone was cool as ice.

Nathan wasn't going to engage, not when she was so mad with him. He stood up, reaching for her hand then stopping when she snatched it away before he even came close to connecting with her.

"I know that you're hurting right now, but I'm not the one you should be angry at. I get that this was a special spot for you and Jock, because he told me so, and if he were here right now he'd tell you himself that you're acting crazy. We rode up here almost every day together."

A look passed over her face that he couldn't read, but the anger disappeared from her eyes like a light going out. He understood that the place was special to her—the wooded hill area tucked away from the rest of the property was like a little slice of paradise hidden away from the world. *Somewhere she was obviously used to enjoying in privacy.* But he hadn't done anything wrong, and grieving or not, he wasn't going to let her take it out on him. If there was one thing her granddad had taught him, it was that just because you were grieving you didn't have leave to behave badly.

"He told you that?" Her voice was softer now. "That it was our special place?"

"Yeah, he did," Nathan replied. "Now why don't you sit down and we can talk, if you're done being angry with me?"

She didn't apologize but she did look guilty, and he wasn't going to rub salt into open wounds. He knew what it was like to lose someone.

"I didn't think anyone else had been here, which I guess is kind of stupid," Jessica said, wiping the corners of her eyes as she sat down across from him amongst the pine needles. "We started coming here when I was a girl, and it was kind of our thing. He always rode Patch, and I was on my old pony, Whiskers."

Nathan nodded, sitting down beside her and stretching his legs back out. He watched as she grimaced, obviously trying to make herself comfortable, but he didn't say anything.

"I hear you had a pretty good hideout, too. Something about a fort that you thought your mom never knew about up in the trees."

Jessica met his gaze, laughed softly and shook her head. "Now I know you're not lying," she said, "because I still believe that no one else knew about *that* little hideaway."

He held his hand to his chest. "Cross my heart, I won't tell another soul."

She leaned back and stared at the horses, and Nathan did the same.

"Patch must be so old now. He was perfect for my granddad, like they understood exactly what the other was thinking. I've never seen anyone else ride him, not ever." She sighed. "That's why it hit me so bad, seeing you. He's been on the farm since I was a little girl."

Nathan chuckled. "Yeah, which is why he's perfect for me. He's content just to take things slow and teach a newbie the ropes." He paused, watched her, wished he didn't feel so uncomfortable being so close to her. "We came up here a lot, the two of us, just to ride and chat, talk about anything and everything. It was as good for me as it was for the old man."

Jessica groaned when she turned to her side, and he waited a second before saying anything more. It was none of his business, but he'd heard so much about her, knew about what had happened, and she was clearly in pain. Jock had been a good friend to him, a mentor, and he missed him more than she could ever imagine. Which meant that he wanted to help Jessica, if he could get past his own demons long enough to do so.

"Sounds like you were close friends. I shouldn't have reacted so badly. I'm sorry."

Nathan frowned at the grimace she was sporting. "From what Jock said, you're supposed to be resting for the next few months, right? As in no getting back in the saddle?" Maybe he wasn't so good at keeping his thoughts to himself.

Jessica didn't shoot him the dagger-filled look he'd been expecting, but she did meet his gaze. "It's stupid, I know, but I just needed to get out in the fresh air and ride. Take it easy, just not in the way my doctor prescribed."

"It's not stupid to want to ride, but you need to let

your body heal." He paused. "After what you went through..."

"You know all about my fall? What happened?" she asked.

He nodded. There was no point pretending otherwise. "The whole country knows all about it. They played the footage from the Badminton Horse Trials over and over on the news, the headlines were screaming about the downfall of New Zealand's eventing golden girl and the best horse this country has ever produced."

Fresh tears were visible in her eyes now, ready to fall. Maybe a simple yes would have been enough— he knew how much she loved her horse, from what Jock had told him, and the equine's career was most definitely over, forever, even if hers wasn't.

"And now my horse is stuck back in the UK, and I'm all useless and back here on my own." Her voice was barely a whisper. "I wish I'd never taken him over, that I'd just campaigned a European horse. I know it sounds stupid, but he's the most incredible animal and I miss him.'

"Is there anything I can do to help?"

Jessica shrugged and stood up, grimacing as she moved. Nathan jumped to his feet and held out a hand to help her, which she took, taking a moment to steady herself. The warm touch of her palm gliding into place alongside his took him by surprise, even though he was the one to initiate it.

"Just a leg up into the saddle would be great," she told him, stopping to give Patch a pat before reaching for the reins of her own mount. "God only knows if I'll ever be able to get up from the ground again on my own."

Nathan bent and took her knee into his palm, counted to three then hoisted her up in the air. She landed gracefully in the saddle, her back beautiful and straight despite how much pain she must have been in. He knew she'd had a back injury, as well as doing some pretty major damage to one of her legs, but he didn't want to pry.

"Nathan, I'm sorry for the way I acted before. I'm not usually so horrible."

He chuckled. "Good, because otherwise I'd have to think your grandfather was a liar. He made you out to be the perfect granddaughter."

Jessica laughed and he found himself grinning straight back at her. There was something so broken about her, so fragile, but at the same time seeing her sit up there in the saddle showed how strong she was, too. She was torn apart, emotionally and physically, but definitely not broken. *Kind of like him.* Only being around her was forcing him to come out of his shell, to be the stronger one, when recently he'd felt so lost, so weak.

"What's that old saying about rose-tinted glasses?" she asked, still smiling.

Nathan laughed. "Mind if I ride back down with you, or do you want some time alone?"

"Sure thing. It's about time I started saying yes to company instead of pretending like I'm better off on my own."

Nathan tried to mount as gracefully as he could and failed terribly, but thankfully Jessica was either too polite to say anything or she actually hadn't noticed. He might be able to *stay* in the saddle, but that was about the extent of it.

"Not bad getting to ride alongside world eventing's number two rider," he joked.

"Well it's a title I'm fast going to lose, so you'd better take the chance while you can."

She was attempting to make fun of what happened, he got that, but he knew she was heartbroken over the accident. Jock had opened up to him about a lot of things, especially about Jessica, and he knew he had to tread carefully. The only thing her grandfather hadn't made clear was how beautiful she was in real life—the photos in the media didn't do her justice. Every time he'd seen her interviewed she'd either been wearing a helmet or had her hair pulled back into a tight bun, dressed in formal riding attire. But with her long blond hair loose, and wearing jeans and a T-shirt, she looked like a different woman. Only he had to keep reminding himself who she was, that she was Jock's granddaughter. Nathan wasn't ready for anything more than a bit of fun, and that wasn't a category that Jessica Falls belonged in. Not ever. If he hadn't been so close to her grandfather, he would have let that be her decision, but it wasn't. Jock had been too important to him, which meant he wasn't going to even think about Jessica like that.

And the truth was, Nathan didn't know if he'd ever be able to commit to any kind of relationship again after what had happened to his wife, which meant nothing could ever happen between them. But it had been a while since he'd had any female company whatsoever, and Jessica wasn't exactly hard to be around, or to look at, even if she was grieving. And looking was entirely different from letting anything happen.

CHAPTER TWO

"So tell me what you're doing in New Zealand."

Jessica slowly rubbed her horse down, paying careful attention to brushing his sweat marks. She would usually have been more vigorous, but her back was starting to ache and she didn't want to push her body too hard, especially since the most strenuous activity she was supposed to be doing was moving from the sofa to the kitchen. The pain was bearable most of the time, unless she overdid it, and then it would hit her like a ton of bricks.

She glanced over at Nathan, watching as he stroked Patch's face. The horse was leaning in to him like they were old friends, and she felt terrible all over again for being so rude to him when she'd found him on the trail. She'd had no right to accuse him of…she didn't even know what.

"I needed some time out from my job and I'd heard how beautiful it was here," he said, looking up but still scratching Patch.

"So you just jumped on a plane and ended up in New Zealand?"

He chuckled. "Yeah, something like that."

She'd been joking, but it seemed she wasn't far off the mark. "So is it everything it's made out to be?"

Nathan put down the brush he'd been holding and walked out of the box stall. "I did the whole touristy thing when I first arrived, but then I found this place a few months ago and I still haven't left."

Jessica untied her horse and nodded to Nathan to do the same with Patch.

"So you've been holed up here with just an old man and some horses for company?" she joked.

Nathan laughed. "Something like that. I've been working my way through a stack of DVD's, staying out of trouble."

"Sounds like exactly what I need to be doing."

"Says the woman who's out riding horses instead of resting up on doctor's orders."

She smiled as they walked through the barn leading the horses out into the open. It was nice to just chat with someone, feel relaxed, even if she did feel guilty for being happy without her granddad around. Her emotions were all over the show right now, and so was her mood, but there was something about Nathan that was drawing her to him.

After letting the horses loose and watching them trot across the field, Jessica and Nathan walked side by side in the direction of the barn again, and Jessica slung her halter and lead rope over her shoulder. At least being home had calmed her, made her feel connected to something again. She was always more settled when she was around horses.

"So it's a different pace of life for you here?" she asked.

"Yeah, you could say that." He looked across at her, his expression more serious, the smile that had braced his lips earlier completely gone. "I had a job I thought I loved, but I was so caught up in working every waking hour that I lost sight of what was important."

Jessica sensed a sadness within him, something that she couldn't quite figure out. There had to be a reason he'd flown halfway across the world, just leaving behind whatever he had in the UK, which meant she was either right about him hurting, or he'd done something he regretted. Or maybe she was just over-thinking the whole situation.

"What type of work did you do?" Jessica asked.

"I was a banker," he said. "I managed a private hedge fund, and I was more married to my work than I was to..." His voice trailed off. "To anything else in my life."

She waited for him to continue but he didn't, leaving her wondering exactly what he was referring to.

"Are you expecting anyone?" he asked.

Jessica glanced toward the driveway, saw an unfamiliar black vehicle approaching the house. *Great.*

"I have a feeling that's the lawyer," she said, fighting the urge to get back on a horse and flee in the opposite direction. "Which means I have to face up to reality instead of hiding away for the next few days." She hadn't expected him to turn up on her doorstep quite so promptly—a day to settle in would have been nice.

"Anything I can do?" The concern in Nathan's voice was matched by his gaze, his bright blue eyes telling her that he genuinely cared.

"How about you come over for a drink tonight." The words left her mouth before she'd even had a moment to think.

The worry lines turned into smile wrinkles when he looked at her this time. "Why don't I grab something for us to eat and bring it over? You can't have much in the pantry, and I doubt you'll have time to get groceries. Lawyers take forever to go over wills."

Jessica braved a smile. It wasn't the will she was worried about—she knew her granddad had left her everything—it was the debts she'd inherited that the lawyer would be wanting her to deal with. Debts he'd been more than eager to contact her about even when she'd been in hospital.

But she did kind of want to see Nathan again. "Dinner sounds great." Her stomach was rumbling just at the thought of food, even though she'd hardly been interested in eating since her accident, and then since Jock had died.

Nathan touched her shoulder, tentatively, his touch light, as if he wasn't sure if it was the right thing to do or not. "Don't let him push you around, and if you need a sounding board, I'm right here."

"Thanks," she said, fighting the urge to shrug his hand away and at the same time wishing he'd never take it off her.

"Your granddad and I talked about everything,

so if you need someone, it's not an empty offer." He smiled at her. "You can trust me."

Jessica wanted to know more, wanted to know why and how he'd become so close to her only family member in the months before he'd died, but now wasn't the time. Tonight she'd try to find out everything she needed to know.

"See you around six?" she asked.

Nathan nodded and withdrew his hand, shoving it in his pocket instead and leaving her wishing he was still touching her, that the heat from his palm was still resting on her shoulder. He might be a stranger, but the physical contact had been oddly comforting.

"See you then," he called out.

Jessica walked briskly toward the house, eyes trained on the man now standing at her front door, waiting. She didn't know why, but she had a strange feeling about the lawyer she'd only ever spoken to on the phone. It was an uneasy notion, a niggle of worry in her mind that she couldn't shake, and she needed to forget all about her curiosity about Nathan and focus on her granddad's state of affairs.

The farm meant everything to her, and if it came to it she wasn't going to give up the property without one hell of a fight. It was her last tie to her family—to her mom and now her granddad—and that made it the most important thing in her life.

"So you're telling me that my only option is to sell this place?"

Jessica stared at the lawyer, listening to what he

was saying but finding it almost impossible to process. She was trying hard not to cry, refusing to admit that there was no other option, but from what he was saying it was almost impossible *not* to admit defeat. Her entire body was numb.

"Your granddad didn't make the wisest decisions over the past year, Ms. Falls. I'm sorry to be the bearer of bad news."

His tone was grave, but he hardly met her gaze, wouldn't hold eye contact for more than a moment and she didn't like him at all now. She also didn't believe that Jock would have left her in such a bad financial position, that the man she'd spent her entire life looking up to could have lost so much in such a short time. It just wasn't right, especially given how cautious and successful he'd been in the past.

"And you're certain there hasn't been, I don't know, some sort of mistake? That there isn't other property or money?" She stood, fidgeting too much to stay seated. "There must be something, or at least some sort of explanation."

Jessica turned to look out the window, looking at the land that she was going to be forced to part with. She had nothing—no job, no future doing what she'd trained for her entire life, and now no inheritance. Every horse, every blade of grass, *everything* about the farm meant more to her than she could ever explain to anyone. Except for her granddad. He'd turn in his grave if he knew she was being forced to sell, which was why nothing about this situation seemed right to her.

"Ms. Falls?"

She was about to turn, to focus her attention back on the lawyer, when a movement caught her eye. *Nathan.* Her mysterious guest was crossing the yard, heading for her back door rather than the main front one, and he was carrying two large brown paper bags. She smiled for the first time since she'd stepped inside. If anyone could help her understand what had happened in the weeks and months before her granddad had passed, it was Nathan. She knew they'd been close, and from what she'd learned today, they'd spent a lot of time together.

"I need a few days to process all this," Jessica said as she turned, squaring her shoulders and staring the lawyer straight in the eyes. She could have been imagining it, but she was certain he looked uncomfortable.

"My advice would be to list the property for sale immediately and consider how to mitigate your losses."

She gave a curt nod and planted her hands on the desk, the coolness of the oak beneath her palms helping to calm her, taking strength from the piece of furniture she'd so often seen her grandfather sit behind.

"Once again, I appreciate your advice, but I'll be taking a few days to consider my options."

The more she could find out from Nathan, the better. But that wasn't the only reason she wanted to see him. There was something about the man that intrigued her, something unassuming about the stranger who'd befriended her granddad that made her want to know more. He was hiding something behind his quiet smile, she just knew it, and she wanted to know what it was.

"I'll see myself out," she heard the lawyer mutter, clearly frustrated with her. He'd probably expected her to admit defeat and sign anything he waved in front of her.

Jessica squared her shoulders, even though her back ached from simply standing so straight after she'd been on her feet all day. Men like this lawyer might think she was weak, that she'd been through so much recently that she'd lost her strength, but mentally she was more determined than ever. To get back in the saddle—which she'd already done—to compete again one day, and most of all to make her grandfather proud and continue his legacy. So she wasn't going to let this lawyer, or any other man, walk all over her. She'd made her mind up years ago that she was in charge of her own destiny, and she needed to hold on to that belief no matter what life threw her way.

"How long did you say you'd been working for Jock?" she asked, her tone cool.

He stopped, briefcase clasped in one hand, the other fisted at his side. She didn't trust him at all. Her grandfather hadn't acquired this farm and a handful of commercial investments without being smart.

"Ah, for some time now. I'd have to consult my records to be absolutely certain."

She nodded and watched him leave. If her intuition was right, she shouldn't trust this man or anyone else until she'd figured out what her grandfather's state of mind had been before he died. If there was one thing he'd taught her, it was to trust only herself in life.

Nathan had seen Jessica in the office when he'd walked past, but he hadn't acknowledged her, instead letting himself in and sitting in the kitchen so he wasn't disturbing her. The oversize wooden table was bathed in sunlight, and he was nursing a beer when Jessica finally walked in to join him. He'd thought about not turning up, or leaving a note with the takeout food and leaving, but he'd made himself stay. It was time to start facing up to reality and stop hiding away, even if that did seem like mission impossible to him right now.

"I hope you don't mind," he said, raising the glass bottle.

Her smile reminded him of a look his wife had once given him, years ago, when they'd first met, and it surprised him by making him smile straight back at her. She looked a combination of exhausted and determined, but she also looked happy to see him.

"You can drink the lot," she told him, opening and shutting the fridge, then disappearing from sight. She reemerged with a bottle of wine. "This is more my taste."

He watched as she searched a few drawers for an opener.

"I think you'll find it's a screw top," he said in a low voice, grimacing when she glared at him.

"You've got to be kidding me." Jessica frowned then shook her head. "I can't even open a bottle of wine. This is definitely not my day. Un-freaking-believable."

Nathan jumped up, leaving his beer on the table, and leaned over the counter to take the bottle from her. Her determined look had been replaced with one that verged on defeated, and he didn't like it. Whatever the lawyer had said had really taken it out of her. He knew what defeated felt like, and it wasn't an emotion he wanted her to experience.

"Bad meeting?" he asked.

"The worst," she admitted, turning away only to reach for a glass. She set it on the counter. "I've basically spent the last couple of hours listening to some idiot lawyer try to tell me that the one person I admired most in the world, who's looked after me my entire life, had lost his marbles. Either that or he wasn't the astute investor I believed him to be—only I don't buy that theory for a second."

"That's rubbish," Nathan shot straight back, anger flaring within him. "I might have only known Jock a short time, but he was as sharp as a tack right to the end. That makes both theories impossible."

"Really?" Jessica asked, taking the glass of wine he'd poured and taking a long, slow sip. "Do you honestly believe that? You're not just saying it to make me feel better?"

Nathan shook his head and moved back to the table, motioning for her to join him. Her gold-flecked eyes were wide again, locked on his as she crossed the room and sat across from him. She tucked her long hair behind her ears, one hand on the glass, the other palm down on the table. He forced himself to glance away, out the window, to stop from staring. There was no denying she was beautiful, even if he was trying not to think about her like that—she was strikingly feminine yet at the same time fiercely strong. And something about that drew him to her as much as it made him want to walk straight out the door.

"Jock was old, but his memory never wavered. We must have spent hours talking every day, and if we weren't just shooting the breeze talking, he was teaching me about horses," he told her.

She sighed and took another sip. "So you're telling me I shouldn't believe the lawyer? That I could be right?"

"I'm telling you that you need to trust yourself." Nathan leaned forward and nudged the bags of food in Jessica's direction. "So how about we eat and you tell me what this so-called lawyer's been saying." He was pleased they had something to focus on while they ate—it took some of the pressure off.

Her gaze shifted, moving to the takeout he'd brought. "How many dishes did you order?"

Nathan grinned straight back at her. "I had no idea what you liked, so I went for Chinese and chose a little of everything."

Jessica was still smiling when she started poking around, taking cartons out and looking inside. "I'm thinking we'll both have enough leftovers to keep us in food for a week."

He liked her easy smile, the way she'd gone from not trusting him to confiding in him, and it was as if he already knew her. After hearing so much about her from Jock, he'd been wanting to meet her, and that was before he'd realized how gorgeous she would be. Not to mention he'd been expecting someone a little more…broken. Jessica might be in pain, might have almost died and ended her career, but she didn't look anything close to broken to Nathan. The fiery blonde was all bent out of shape over whatever the lawyer had said to her, and he wanted to know more. Because if he could help, there was nothing he wouldn't do, not when it meant helping the granddaughter of the man who'd brought him back from the brink and made him believe he at least had a future ahead of him. He had a long way to go, but life wasn't as dark as it had seemed when he'd first arrived.

She held up the throwaway chopsticks and broke them apart then pulled a lid off one dish, expertly helping herself to noodles like she was as used to using them as he was a knife and fork.

"So what do you think of this place?"

Her question took him by surprise. "I wouldn't have stayed so long if I didn't love it."

Her sigh made him look up, forgetting what he'd been about to eat.

"Why?" he asked.

She met his gaze, eyes dull as she opened her mouth to answer him. He tried not to stare at her lips, at the way they moved when she blew out a breath.

"Because from what the lawyer's telling me, it'll

be on the market before the end of the month, so I might need a buyer. You interested?"

He put down his chopsticks. "You're serious?" He'd realized things were bad, that Jock's affairs obviously hadn't been left in order, but to sell the place?

"Deadly," she answered straight back.

He had no idea what to say. "You're sure that's something you have to consider?"

"Honestly?" She shook her head, tears making her big brown eyes look like they were swimming. "I hope not, but from what I heard tonight I don't know what else I'll be able to do."

Nathan picked up a spring roll between his fingers and dipped it in sauce, slowly eating it as he digested her words.

"If it comes to selling, if it's what you have to do, I'll buy the place myself."

She laughed. "Yeah, right."

Nathan cleared his throat and looked up, not wanting to sound arrogant but needing her to know it wasn't an empty offer. That he could buy it tomorrow and come up with the cash immediately if he had to. "I'm serious."

Her laughter died, the uneasy smile wiped from her face. She studied him, eyes no longer full of tears—her gaze was serious now. "You could actually buy this place, just like that?" she asked.

He shrugged, not wanting to make a big deal out of it. A year ago, hell, a few months ago, he'd have had no problem letting anyone know what he could afford, but since coming here…he just didn't want to be that guy anymore. Staying on the farm had given him the break he'd needed, and it had also given him a fresh start, even if he was going to have to face reality and head home one day soon.

"Yeah, I could. But if I did I'd need a manager, so there's no chance I'd evict you."

Jessica smiled, but he knew she wasn't sure what to say or how to take his words.

"But it won't come to that, so don't even worry," he assured her.

She took another mouthful of noodles and nodded, but he sensed the change in her, as if she was suddenly viewing him as a stranger when before she'd treated him like an ally. Money attracted a lot of women—the wrong women—but he doubted Jessica fell into that category, even if she was desperate for an injection of cash to save her assets. If she did, her eyes would have lit up, her smile would have become wider—he knew all the signs—and yet she'd looked more alarmed than anything else. She could just be good at hiding her emotions, but she'd been so honest about her grief that he doubted it.

"So you said you're a banker, when you're not traveling?"

"I was, back in London," he said, taking the lid off another dish. "I managed a private hedge fund."

"Ahh, I see," she said, like finding out what he did told her everything she needed to know.

It felt like a lifetime ago to him, and in some ways it was. The guy he was here was nothing like the man he'd been for most of his adult life.

"So will you go back? To being a banker?"

It was something he'd thought about a lot lately, and he still wasn't sure. "That life took everything from me," he said, pushing the memories away that were trying to claw their way back in, the memories that so often took hold of him and refused to give him any relief. "I need to go back at some point, but right now I'm happy pretending to be someone else."

The smile she gave him this time lit her eyes again, as if she was happy with his answer. "So does the person you are here have time to help me figure out what the hell happened to my inheritance?"

Nathan grinned. It had been a long time since he'd hung out and chatted to a beautiful woman—he couldn't even recall the last time he'd chilled out and eaten take-out food with his wife. This was the type of evening he'd missed out on over the past decade, what he'd thought was overrated. Now he knew otherwise. And it had also been a while since he'd been able to really use his brain, and if he was honest with himself he kind of missed that part of his old life.

"It just so happens that I'm great with numbers, so if you need me to look at any transactions, bank accounts, anything, I'm your guy."

At times like this, he knew his old lifestyle hadn't been worth what he'd lost, the memories he'd have to live with for the rest of his life. He'd tried so hard to have everything, and all he'd done was lose what he'd spent years striving for. Jessica was like a breath of fresh air, even if she was in need of his help. So long as he kept reminding himself that she could be only a friend, he'd be just fine. Because not only was she Jock's granddaughter, she was also an attractive woman, and part of being away from home was about keeping his life complication free.

Jessica was vulnerable right now, and he wasn't going to take advantage of that. Although if there was something he could do to help her, he would. "So tell me what the lawyer said."

She rolled her eyes and took another mouthful before leaning back in her chair, anger taking over her face again.

"You know, when I met you earlier, I told myself to be nice to you because you were a paying guest."

He chuckled, curious. "And now?"

Her dark eyes locked on his. "Now?" she shrugged. "Now I think that I was a little harsh. I can't be an island forever."

"An island?" He had no idea what she was talking about, but she had a great knack of taking his mind from his thoughts.

"Let's just say that I usually keep to myself. I've always been a loner."

Nathan didn't know if she was just being friendly or if she was flirting with him. He'd been married for half of his twenties and part of his thirties, and even if he hadn't been he'd worked almost every waking hour since he'd graduated, which meant he'd been out of the game for way too long. So darn long that he couldn't even figure out if Jessica was interested or just being friendly.

"For the record, I'm pleased you've given up the whole island thing."

She laughed. "Yeah?"

So much for not flirting. He'd even managed to throw a dumb joke in there, or at least his pitiful attempt at a joke.

"So tell me what it's like being a banker," she asked between mouthfuls.

Nathan refused to be drawn back into the past, to let himself think too much about what she'd just asked him. But Jessica knew nothing about what had happened; she was just asking an innocent question. It wasn't her fault that just the mention of his past brought back memories so vivid, a gut-wrenching pain so deep, that it seemed like he could choke just trying to breath.

"In my first year one of the other interns died from staying awake almost 24/7 and working insane hours," he told her, watching as her jaw physically dropped, mouth gaping open. "The poor guy was so fatigued, had worked a few days straight, and he had a heart attack."

"You're kidding me. Please tell me you're kidding."

"I wish I was," he said with a grimace. "The kind of industry I was in, it took a lot from plenty of us, but the game of what we do is so addictive that sometimes it takes something pretty major to jolt us out."

Her eyebrows bunched together as she stared at him. "And a young guy dying didn't alert you to the kind of job you were getting yourself into *before* you'd committed?"

Nathan shrugged. It was something he'd asked himself so many times after he'd lost his wife, but he knew the answer. The truth was that nothing could have made him give up his job back then—the money had been too good and he'd loved what he did each day—until he'd found his wife. He blinked a few times in fast succession, as if it would make the memories magically disappear. And the way his family were, their expectations; they had almost made his career decision for him. But he wasn't about to talk to her about his family, because that would be going back in time to something else he was only too happy to forget.

"That's why I'm here," he told her. "It took me a while, years, but I finally realized that there was a life for me away from Mayfair. I just had to leave London to figure that out." *If only it hadn't taken him so long.* "I lost someone I loved, and it made me rethink—" he paused "—everything. But I know that if I was twenty-one all over again, nothing anyone could have said to me would have made a difference."

Jessica's face was soft, her expression kind as she watched him. "Sometimes it takes losing what we love to show us how much that person or thing meant to us in the first place," she said, her voice low, almost husky. "I've spent my entire life looking up to the world's best riders, and then when I finally achieved my dreams I lost everything."

He didn't know what to tell her, because nothing he could say would change how she felt. He still hadn't come to terms with what had happened to him, which meant there was no way in hell she would in the near future, either.

"I bet every second person tells you that it'll get better. That you'll learn to deal with what's happened."

Jessica slowly nodded, running her fingertips across the wooden surface of the table. "The only way I'll come to terms with what happened to me is when I'm out competing again."

He sensed there was something else, that she was holding something back. Jessica was staring past him; he guessed she was looking through the window even though the light was fading fast and it was almost dark. She was keeping secrets, just like he was.

"And then there's Teddy."

Nathan knew instantly who she was talking about, because he'd read all the news stories about her when it had happened. She hadn't mentioned her horse, so he hadn't asked, but from the way she was biting down on her bottom lip, tears glinting in her eyes, he was guessing the outcome wasn't good.

"Did he, ah, recover from his injuries in the end?" He tried not to grimace, worried he'd said the wrong thing and not wanting to upset her.

Jessica poured herself another glass of wine, sighing and taking a large sip before looking back up. "I'll never be able to compete him again, but he means the world to me, Nathan. He deserves a retirement here on the farm, going for a ride every now and again if he's not too stiff, even just being in the field with a few of the youngsters to keep them company." Her voice was shaky. "I just want him with me."

"So where is he?"

Her eyebrows pulled together, frustration clear on her face. "He's still stuck in the UK. I don't know if I'll ever be able to raise the money to bring him back now, which means I'll—" she closed her eyes for a moment, taking a visibly deep breath "—have to have him put down. He's worthless to anyone else, and I won't be able to afford the livery for long, if at all."

Nathan could feel her pain, could see how upset she was talking about an animal she so clearly loved. He reached for her across the table, covered her hand with his before even thinking about what he was doing. Nathan squeezed her fingers, wondering what the hell he was doing as he looked into her eyes. It was almost painful just touching her, connecting with another human being, but he forced himself not to pull away.

"How much do you need to fly him home?" he asked.

She shifted her hand beneath his but didn't remove it. "Too much," she replied, voice soft.

Nathan slowly took his fingers from hers, sliding them away and reaching for his beer. But that wasn't why he'd withdrawn—her skin, so soft and warm, was making him think how much he wanted to keep touching her. How much he'd missed being with a woman, or even just being close to any other person.

"Find out how much and I'll take care of it."

Her eyes went wide, round like saucers. "No." She shook her head like she was trying to convince herself otherwise. "Absolutely not."

"Why not?" If it meant that much to her, he'd pay the bill without a second thought. "Your granddad meant a lot to me, so just think of it as my way of repaying him."

"No matter how much he did for you, he wouldn't let you spend thirty grand on bringing a retired horse home."

Nathan chuckled and raised an eyebrow. "I thought you didn't know how much it cost."

She shrugged. "That's the rough price, but honestly? There's no way I could ever afford it, not now, and I'm not taking handouts from anyone." Jessica sighed. "Besides, this place won't even be here then. I'm going to have to sell, which means I won't even have somewhere to keep him or any of the others. I have to face the cold, hard facts."

Nathan stared long and hard at the grim set of her mouth and the sad look in her eyes. It was almost like looking at a reflection of himself, of the way he felt so often. "Look, if you want him back I'll pay, no strings attached. And I want to make it clear that I'll buy Patch if it comes to that, and I'll pay for somewhere nice to stable him if I need to, for as long as he needs it."

Jessica's expression changed, her eyes soft, the faintest lines appearing at the corners as she smiled at him. "Thank you," she said. "That old horse means a lot to me, too."

Nathan resisted the urge to reach for her again, but the way she was looking at him made it almost impossible. There was something about being in New

Zealand that had changed his outlook, made him appreciate the more simple things he'd taken for granted most of his life, but until now he'd also appreciated the time on his own. Or maybe he'd just been terrified of ever letting anyone close again. Now? He knew he'd been traveling solo for long enough, but even the thought of Jessica's beautiful smile didn't make it easier for him to think about…what? He didn't even know what. He only knew that he liked her, and that she made him want to push past what had been holding him back for so long.

"So you'd let me buy him?"

"If it comes to that, yes." This time her smile was determined instead of kind when she flashed it. "But I like to win my own battles, Nathan, and that means I don't want to be anyone's charity case."

From the look on her face she'd been offended by his offer when all he'd been trying to do was help. "So I can help you with one horse, but not the other?" He should have kept his mouth shut but the words just slipped out before he could help it.

"The difference is that you genuinely like Patch. He means a lot to you and you're attached to him. But if I let you help me with Teddy then I'd owe you a debt I could never repay." She laughed, but it was more of a nervous chuckle. "Besides, I've never wanted to be some rich man's bought-and-paid-for mistress."

This time he should have said something, but he only stared at her. All his life he'd been surrounded by people impressed by wealth, seen women flock to

rich men, and here Jessica was rebuffing him immediately *because* of his money. *Money she desperately
needed.* It shouldn't have mattered to him, but something about her words only made him more intrigued.
Made him want to help her all the more, a challenge
that he couldn't ignore. And a challenge that made
him forget all about his demons, at least for the moment. Or maybe it was the comment about being his
mistress that had shocked him into forgetting.

"You know, I think we kind of got off track," he
finally said, breaking the silence.

She only raised her eyebrows in response.

"Tonight was supposed to be about cheap and
cheerful food and a few drinks," he continued.

"And you helping me solve the mystery of my
grandfather's demise," she added, smile back on her
face.

"Let me look through all Jock's paperwork in the
morning," Nathan suggested, wanting an excuse to
see her again as much as he wanted to help. "If there's
one thing I can do, it's figure out if anyone's swin-
dled the old man."

Jessica held up her now half-empty wine glass.
"I'll drink to that."

Nathan raised his beer bottle and met her stare,
surprised that she held his gaze instead of looking
away. Earlier in the day she'd hardly been able to
look at him, had seemed more annoyed than anything
that he'd stopped by to introduce himself, and now
her smile alone was warming a part of him that had

been cold for the better part of the last year. A part of him that he'd thought would never heal.

"So tell me about this gorgeous old horse of yours," he said.

"Hey, who're you calling old?"

Jessica stood at the door and watched as Nathan walked slowly backward. She raised her hand in a wave, before crossing both arms over her chest, more for comfort than for the cold. It was weird spending time with someone who knew so much about her, but who was essentially still a stranger. Weird but nice at the same time.

"Thanks for coming over," she said, leaning against the doorjamb

Nathan stopped, hands pushed into his pockets. "So tomorrow we start investigating?" he asked.

"Maybe we should go for a ride," she suggested, liking the idea of anything that meant she got to spend extra time with him.

"Sounds good. I'll see you tomorrow."

She stared after him, watching as he went part way down the drive before crossing over the lawn and heading for the cottage. So much for wishing she didn't have a guest to deal with. Spending time with Nathan had pulled her from her own miserable thoughts, stopped her from wallowing in what had happened and what could happen in the near future. And it had made her more determined.

Jessica shut the door and headed for the kitchen, sighing as she looked at the table where they'd been sitting. There wasn't much to clean up, just a couple of beer bottles, the take-out containers and her wineglass, and then she needed to head to bed. Although no matter how tired she was, the jet lag making her entire body fatigued, she knew sleep wouldn't come easily. Not tonight.

As she collected the bottles and put them in her recycling container, she thought of Nathan, and then her granddad. One man was making her body tingle, making her wish she'd never been so snappy with him earlier in the day, and the other...he was making her worry. Worry about losing the last thing in her life that truly meant something to her. She'd grown up without her dad, but Jock had been the only male role model she'd ever needed. Her mom had been amazing one moment and downbeat the next, and she tried so hard not to think about her sometimes, because it only brought back memories of losing her. Of what had happened. How traumatic her death had been.

Jessica pushed the thoughts away and left the kitchen, deciding to finish cleaning up in the morning, and headed for the stairs. She looked up, ready to collapse into bed when a sliver of light caught her eye. She'd left the light on in the office by mistake, but she took it as a sign.

Jessica looked up the stairs one last time, groaned then padded barefoot to the office, stretching her back as she walked. She might be tired, but she was also on the cusp of losing the farm. She had the rest of her life to sleep and only a short time to save what she loved. She just had to remember to make time for her exercises, because if she let her back seize up and not heal, she'd become too stiff to ever get back in the saddle again. And a life without riding would be a life not worth living.

CHAPTER THREE

JESSICA GRIMACED AS SHE stretched her body out, holding the yoga pose even though it was killing her. She pushed out a big breath then inhaled again as she slowly released, before forcing her body to comply again. What she needed was a hot yoga class to go to, but she doubted there was anything local—she'd have to travel at least an hour and she didn't have the time. Same with acupuncture—she would have loved a session, but she wasn't keen on letting just anyone stick needles into her.

"That looks painful."

She froze, shutting her eyes for a second. *Nathan.* She hadn't expected him to be about so early, let alone to be dropping in to see her. When she relaxed out of her pose and opened her eyes, she looked up at him and saw that he was dressed in workout gear, too.

"Painful would be an understatement," she replied, slowly stretching out and standing. "But if I ever want my old body back, I'm prepared to deal with the consequences."

His low laugh made her smile. "That's how I felt

when I started back running. It's been ten years since I pounded the pavements around London, and I'm finally getting fit again."

"Another perk of quitting your job?" she asked, reaching for her water and taking a long sip.

"Something like that."

They stood and stared at one another for a moment, until Jessica put down her bottle. There was something awkward about having Nathan so close, about him staying on the property—awkward but nice at the same time. And she could tell that even though he was friendly, that he wanted to be around her, too, he was finding the whole thing as awkward as she was.

"I'd ask you in for breakfast but I don't really have anything to offer." It was the truth—some bread in the freezer was all she had to eat, which meant she was going to have to do a trip to the supermarket if she didn't want to starve. "You could join me for yoga, but that's about as good as it gets."

Nathan stared at her as if he was deep in thought before he said anything. "How about you give me five minutes for a shower and come over to the cottage? I'm on a serious health kick right now, so my refrigerator is jam-packed with food."

She glanced down at her workout gear and touched her ponytail, running her fingers through it. It was a beautiful morning: the sun was already shining bright across the lawn and filtering onto the porch, and there was nothing she'd rather do than sit with Nathan and eat something other than toast. If she could shower first, that was—it had been a long night and she felt terrible.

"Give me half an hour," she said, smiling at him. "Breakfast would be lovely."

As he turned to walk away, she called out to him. "Hey, if you're on a health kick, how did we end up eating greasy noodles and spring rolls last night?"

The grin he gave her made her wish she didn't have so much other crap going on that she had to deal with. That she could just enjoy flirting with a handsome guy instead of stressing about every other aspect of her life. Although given what she was going through, maybe he was the perfect distraction.

"I'm allowed the odd treat day," he told her. "And besides, you looked like you needed comfort food."

She rolled up her yoga mat instead of staring after him as he disappeared, but she couldn't wipe the smile from her face. A morning of not dealing with reality wasn't going to kill her, and besides, she was starving. Now she just had to move at lightening speed to shower and get ready.

After what felt like the fastest half hour of her life, Jessica wandered across the grass toward the cottage, trying not to hurry and telling herself he wasn't going to notice if she was five minutes late. It had been a long time since she'd seen the little house, and a smile came to her face as she looked at the climbing rose that still covered one side of the wooden structure. It was almost like an oversize kid's playhouse, and it had been the place she'd lived in when she was younger, before her granddad had managed to convince her mom that she was crazy for insisting on being so independent. Then they'd moved into the main house, and this had been used for friends and family, or for guests when Jock had felt like some company over the past few years. She'd always guessed he'd rented the place when he was lonely, as he liked having younger people around him, but now she wondered if he'd needed the extra money. It was all just so frustrating not being able to ask him what the hell had happened.

Jessica inhaled deeply, convinced she could smell coffee but certain she must be imagining it. She ran her fingers through her hair, a nervous habit that she was always prone to whenever she wore it loose. Most of her life she'd worn a ponytail or plait, having worn a helmet almost every day and needing to be practical, but lately she'd liked blow-drying it and leaving it out, one of the only things she'd enjoyed about not training.

"Hey."

She looked up and saw Nathan standing barefoot in the doorway, wearing faded jeans and a white T-shirt. He looked like he was born to live on the farm, relaxed and sporting a smile as casual as his clothing, which made it hard to match him with the banker he'd described. In fact, there was almost nothing about him that would ever have hinted at what his usual life was, except maybe his posh English accent. And that hint of sadness that reflected in his gaze— something she doubted he was even aware that he did—that told her he wasn't as carefree and relaxed as he looked sometimes.

He'd disappeared almost the moment he'd called out, so she just walked slowly to the low porch where the old table was set. She ran her hand along the chair, smiling as she thought about the times she'd sat there in the past. First it had been with her mom, then as somewhere fun to play and have pretend tea parties as a girl, and later it had been a place to sit and think when she'd been a teenager. And when her mom had died, it had been oddly comforting to sit and remember her, sometimes on her own and other times with her granddad silently sitting beside her. Although remembering had always been a lot tougher than trying to forget.

Jessica brushed aside the tears that were pricking her eyes, blinking as she heard Nathan coming out. She didn't need to go back to that night, to the sirens wailing and the lights flashing in the dead of night, the police car arriving to tell her and her granddad what had happened. She'd been so numb from news of the crash that it had passed as a blur, in the beginning anyway. And it just made her more determined not to let anyone too close, so she didn't have to experience that kind of loss again.

"I hope you're not expecting anything too exciting," Nathan said, putting two bowls on the table and standing back. "I've started eating kind of simple food since I've been here."

Jessica looked from him to the table. "Are you serious? What about this is simple?"

The bowls were filled with gourmet muesli, then piled high with every kind of berry. It was exactly what she needed after not looking after herself properly while she'd been overseas, usually too busy riding and making sure her horses got the best of everything, then forgetting about herself. Her go-to food had been grilled cheese and frozen meals—or anything fast when she'd been short on time.

"The farmer's market here is amazing," Nathan said, ignoring her compliment and disappearing inside as he called over his shoulder. "You should come with me tomorrow."

Jessica sat down, using a fork to nudge aside the berries and steal a few blueberries from the bottom. She hadn't eaten them in years, and the sweet tartness made her taste buds explode, flooding her mouth and making her crave more.

She watched Nathan make his way from the door to the table again, holding another bowl. There was no denying how handsome he was—hair tousled and slightly messy, skin tanned no doubt from the hours he'd been spending outside. It was a weird feeling, but there was something nice about knowing that the hours he'd spent on horseback had been with her granddad. That he'd been the person her grandfather had seen everyday.

"This," he said, "is coconut yogurt. Believe me when I tell you it's the best thing you'll ever eat."

Jessica couldn't help but burst out laughing. "Coconut yogurt? Next you're going to tell me that you meditate all day."

"Well," he began, a serious look on his face. Then he grinned straight back at her with a playful expression that masked any hint of sadness. "I'm just trying to stay healthy, that's all. Eating clean food, cooking and exercising, doing the things I neglected for too long." He chuckled. "But I haven't taken up meditation and pilates just yet."

Nathan nudged the yogurt in her direction and she dipped her spoon in, taking his word for how delicious it was going to be. She licked her spoon and then ate the lot, eyes opening wide at the flavor.

"Oh my god, it *is* incredible."

"Told you so," he said, a smug look on his face. "That's the passion fruit one, my favorite. Although it has nothing on the chocolate coconut ice cream."

She took a mouthful of everything together, nodding, as he raised an eyebrow at her. "I think you're on to something with this health kick."

Nathan made a noise in his throat that she couldn't decipher before answering. "A heart attack will do that to a guy."

She almost dropped her spoon. Did he mean him? Surely not. "You mean your father or someone else close to you?"

He shook his head, looking at her from across the table. "Nope. Me."

No way. "But you're like, what? Thirty-something?"

This time he nodded. "Thirty-two. Way too young for a heart attack, but it happened."

Jessica concentrated on her next few mouthfuls,

but she couldn't even remember what they'd been talking about before the whole heart attack thing.

"So what do you say to the market?"

"Market?" she mumbled back, still trying to process what he'd said.

"The farmer's market. Tomorrow."

She sighed. "Sorry, I'm still kind of stuck on the whole heart failure thing."

His eyes met hers, a blend of chocolate warmth and strength that she couldn't look away from. "Now you get why I'm trying to be healthy, though, right? I'm not just trying to stick to some crazy New Year's resolution, I've changed everything. My lifestyle, my attitude, *everything.*"

She finished her mouthful, wanting to know more but not game enough to ask. "The market sounds great. Maybe while we're there you can tell me what I need to shop for. And how to put it all together."

"Just think what cavemen would have eaten, and you'll figure it out pretty quick," he joked.

Jessica fought the urge to stare at Nathan, to study his face. There was something else, something beneath the surface that she couldn't quite figure out. The heart attack was…unbelievable, but she knew there was more to what had happened to him, more than he was telling her. His eyes told of sadness, although when he looked at her like he was now and smiled, that look almost disappeared. *Almost.*

The closer she got to thirty, the more she started to question the fact that it had been so long since she'd been in a relationship. There were only so many times she could blame her distrust in the opposite sex on her deadbeat father, even if deep down she did believe that her trust issues were his fault. Not every man was her ex either—after two years she had to start telling herself that. *And believing it.*

And being with Nathan…maybe it was just that she hadn't met a man she was attracted to in a long time, but being around him it was kind of hard *not* to think about how her body was reacting to his.

When he'd touched her the night before, when his hand had closed over hers, it was as if her skin had come alive, tingling with desire. Now she wanted to reach out to him, to run her fingers down his arm, feel his skin. But she'd missed the moment. She could have done it, could have gotten away with touching him when he'd confessed about his heart attack. Now it would just seem plain weird, and she wasn't even sure about how she felt, what she wanted.

"So are you going to look through any of your granddad's paperwork today? Try to figure out where everything started to go wrong?"

Jessica yawned, though she tried hard to suppress it. "Would you believe me if I said I sat up until almost four a.m. rifling through everything I could find?"

His smile was warm. "Absolutely. I would have done the same."

She put down her spoon, no longer hungry, although she hadn't finished. "I'm starting to think I'm crazy, that the jet lag is doing weird things to my brain, but…" She let her sentence trail off, not wanting to sound like a madwoman. She was doubting herself that she could be right, that her stupid conspiracy theory was exactly that.

"Tell me," he said, setting his spoon down and leaning forward slightly, elbows on the table, like he was waiting for her to divulge some big secret. "I promise I won't laugh."

She fiddled with the edge of her top, picking at the hem absentmindedly. "From the correspondence I could find, it seems that Granddad sold a lot of investment properties over the last year. He didn't use a computer, but he wrote everything in his diary, and he was meeting with his lawyer around the same time as each property was sold. His notes are meticulous."

Nathan's eyebrows shot up before pulling together, causing a crease to appear between them. She tightened her fingers into a fist, resisting the urge to reach out and smooth his skin, to touch his frown away. Part of her wanted to connect with him, and the other part was terrified. And she didn't know whether he might run a mile if she did touch him out of the blue like that.

"He wasn't losing his mind, Jessica, and the notes he made prove it. I think you need to trust your instincts."

"So you don't think I'm crazy for thinking that his lawyer could have—" she paused, considering her words "—taken advantage of him?"

"No, not crazy at all." Nathan stood up, taking both their bowls and nodding toward the kitchen. "There's plenty of things he could have done fraudulently, but the tricky part is figuring out what and then trying to prove it."

She stood too, following him inside and momentarily forgetting what they were talking about when she saw a shiny, state-of-the-art coffee machine taking pride of place in the tiny kitchen.

"I take it caffeine is allowed on your new healthy regime?"

Nathan turned around faster than she expected, almost knocking her over. She took a step back at the same time as he reached for her arm, his hand closing over her elbow to steady her, the look on his face almost alarmed when he realized how close they were, that his skin was covering hers.

"Thanks," she managed, staring up into his coffee-bean-dark eyes. Now that he was standing so close he seemed so tall, so…masculine. Everything about him was making the room seem smaller, making her acutely aware of the fact that she was up close and personal with a man she was most definitely attracted to. She only had to move an inch, push up onto her tiptoes and tilt her head back, and she'd be so close to kissing him, to touching her mouth to his.

"There's nothing wrong with a good, strong coffee," he finally said, staring down at her for what felt like an eternity before letting her go and stepping back.

And there would be nothing wrong with a kiss, either. Jessica shoved her hands in her pockets and looked around the kitchen and small living room.

"How do you like it?"

She spun back around. *How did she like it?* "What?" she asked.

He smiled, the awkwardness disappearing as he laughed. "Your coffee. How do you like it?"

Jessica felt her cheeks burn just enough to make her embarrassed. "Cappuccino. Thanks," she managed, turning her back so he couldn't see her face. "With sugar."

"So back to your sleuthing. Do you think there's any chance your granddad signed a power of attorney over to his lawyer?"

She shut her eyes, trying to recall the conversations she'd had with her granddad in the months before he'd passed. If anything it made her stop thinking about how she felt being around Mr. Tall Dark and Handsome. He had mentioned something about making provision in case something happened to him, but...*yes.* It was all starting to come back to her. "He did."

Nathan fired the coffee machine into life, the hiss of frothing milk making her turn around to watch, curious.

"Then that's where you need to start," he said.

"You think he's blatantly ripped Granddad off? Sold my inheritance out from under me?" Her heart was beating faster just considering the possibility, her body felt as if it was on fire just from her thinking about it. Surely he couldn't have, could he?

Nathan put one coffee cup down before starting on the next, glancing at her as he worked. "It wouldn't be the first time a lawyer did this kind of thing. Honestly?" he said over the noise of the machine. "I think it's a more plausible theory than Jock losing his marbles and selling the investments he'd worked so hard to acquire. I flat out believe that didn't happen."

Jessica took the coffee Nathan offered her, bending to inhale the aroma. "Smells heavenly," she told him.

"There's no decent coffee close by, except for Sundays when the market opens, so I decided to teach myself. It beats driving twenty minutes for one."

She laughed. "And spend a small fortune on a machine."

"There is that. But it's not like I'm spending a lot of money living here."

Jessica already knew her guest wasn't exactly strapped for cash. In fact, if she had to guess, she would bank on him being wealthy even by London standards, and she'd met a lot of people when she was living there with enough money to make her eyes pop. He'd been so quick to insist that he could buy the farm, not to mention offering to write the check to bring Teddy home for her. But she couldn't accept, it just wasn't right, and she didn't want to be that much in debt to anyone.

"You'll get to the bottom of all this. We'll figure it out together, because he's bound to have left a trail, and we just have to follow the crumbs."

"So the saga begins," she muttered, wincing when she touched the side of the hot coffee cup. If her hunch was correct then she was up for one hell of a battle, but it was oddly comforting knowing Nathan was helping her, that she wasn't alone.

* * *

"So tell me what it was like to compete at the World Equestrian Games."

Jessica looked across at Nathan as they walked, tucking her thumbs through the belt loops of her jeans. Part of her didn't want to go back in time, didn't want to remember what it was like, but the other part of her was so determined to get back there one day that she was terrified of losing the memories. Like with her mom—she'd spent so long trying to forget, and then even longer worrying that she wouldn't be able to remember her face if she kept pushing the memories away.

She slowed her walk and went back to gazing across the fields. "It was amazing," she told him. "Experience-of-a-lifetime kind of stuff, and riding alongside some of my childhood idols was incredible."

They strolled along in silence until they reached the yards, large pens that ran alongside the barn. They were empty—she had left all the horses out to graze the night before—but she still hitched one foot up on the wooden rail.

"Will you ever get back there?" Nathan asked, his voice soft and low.

Jessica shut her eyes. Behind her lids she could see herself cantering around the cross-country course, feel the steady beat of Teddy's hooves as they traveled fast toward a jump, soaring through the air and landing clear on the other side. *Yes.* In her heart she couldn't stand the thought of a lifetime without competing, and she wasn't the sort of person to take no for an answer. Screw the doctors and what they had to say. So long as someone would let her campaign their horse, since she wouldn't ever be able to afford her own, she believed she would.

"One day I'll be back there," she said, angling her body so she was facing him. "And even if it is unlikely, I'm not ready to take no for an answer. Not for a long time yet."

Nathan's eyes were fixed on hers, and she would have known he was smiling even if she hadn't been able to see his mouth. His whole face crinkled slightly, his expression warm all the way to his eyes, all awkwardness between them long disappeared, for the moment anyhow.

"You'll get there."

She swallowed hard, goose pimples spreading across her skin as he continued to stare at her, not breaking contact for even a second. She felt her breathing become shallow, anticipation making her body hum; waiting for him to move closer, for something to happen between them. She might be confused about a lot of things, but Nathan kissing her, *touching* her, wasn't one of them. It was the kind of distraction she was craving.

"Jessica…" he started, shuffling forward a little, his gaze moving from her eyes to her mouth then slowly back again.

Her lips parted, staring back at him, waiting. He hovered, seemed to somehow rock forward then back away again. And that was when she noticed it, as his hand moved up slowly, reaching for her face, about to cup her cheek.

Her heart started to beat fast for another reason entirely, her blood feeling as if it were on fire in her veins as it pumped through her body. *He was married?* How had she not noticed the fact that he wore a fine gold band before now?

"You're married," she managed, her voice catching in her throat and sounding all husky when she wanted to sound mad.

Desire was replaced by anger. She had no idea what was going on, but she wanted to know—now. Not that she had any right to demand him share his life story, but if he'd kissed her and then she'd found out he was married? The idea of it made her physically sick. She would never do anything even remotely intimate with a married man, not when she'd seen firsthand the emotional impact of infidelity. It had crippled her mom and she would never let another man close to her, not ever. And then when she'd found out her ex had another partner, was engaged to another woman and had been lying to her for months... Jessica's body shook. *How dare he.*

Nathan took a step away from her, leaning against the rails. "I'm not married, Jessica," he said.

She wanted to scoff at him, to accuse him of lying when she could so blatantly see his ring, but before she could react he held his left hand out and shrugged, rolling the ring around his finger before slipping it off and holding it up to the light, inspecting it. She kept her mouth shut, waiting for him to explain himself.

"Old habits die hard," he muttered, shoving it into his pocket. "I'm a widower, actually. I just don't like to think about it if I can help it."

Jessica wished the ground would open up and swallow her. *A widower?* Now she felt awful. The thought hadn't even crossed her mind. It was the second time she'd jumped to conclusions where Nathan was concerned, and she felt like a fool.

"I, um," she stuttered, not able to take her eyes off him or manage to say anything coherent. "I'm sorry."

He shrugged again, but she could tell she'd hit a raw nerve. Was that another reason why he'd traveled halfway around the world to escape his normal life? It sure explained the sadness she'd kept glimpsing.

"It's been a while, but I guess I'm just so used to wearing it. I should have taken it off months ago."

Jessica nodded, not sure whether to ask him more or just wait for him share if he wanted to. At least now she understood why he'd been so caring, so genuine when she'd been talking about her grandfather. Nathan knew loss like she had, or maybe even more so if he'd lost his wife. Which was no doubt why they'd connected so quickly, why he'd been comfortable talking with her about moving on and things getting better, something most people shied away from.

She wished they could rewind, go back to that moment when something had been so close to happening between them, but it was long gone. Now Nathan was staring into the distance, his mind no doubt a million miles away, and she was feeling numb.

"I might, ah, head back and start sorting through

some more paperwork. Try to figure everything out."
And stop thinking about the fact they'd almost kissed.

Nathan turned, slowly, his expression soft again,
dark eyes suddenly as inviting as warm hot chocolate
on a freezing cold winter's night. When he reached
for her hand, she didn't pull away, instead letting him
hold it as she looked at his golden skin against hers.

"We'll figure all this out, Jessica." He looked as
unsure about touching her as she did about receiv-
ing the affection, but they both stayed still. Stayed
connected.

She smiled, because she trusted what he was saying. "Thank you." Although part of her wondered if
he was talking about her money issues or the attraction simmering between them.

"I'm just going to stay here awhile," he told her.
"See you tomorrow for the market?"

"Sure."

Jessica refused to feel disappointed when he let
go of her hand, when nothing else happened between
them. If something was supposed to happen, if she
was supposed to feel those full lips of his pressed
to hers, she just had to believe it would. *Sometime
when she wasn't accusing him of almost committing
adultery.*

She made her way back toward the house, groaning
at the thought of the papers she had to look through.
But one breath of clean country air, one look at her
surroundings, only made her more determined to get
to the bottom of whatever was going on. And then
once she'd figured all of that out, she needed to fig-

ure out how to get her horse on a plane. Somehow she'd figure it all out. *Somehow.*

Nathan wished he could find a way to start over, but every time he thought he was moving forward, that he was dealing with what had happened, something slapped him right back to where he'd started. And if he was honest with himself, it was Jessica who'd affected him this time, who'd made his memories come tumbling back. Not that he was ever going to forget them, but still—she'd made them worse, but only because of the way he was thinking about her. He'd had a wonderful woman in his life, a woman who'd deserved so much better than him, and he would never forget lifting her body down and holding her, lifeless, wishing he'd been there for her when she'd needed him most. That he hadn't found her with the noose around her neck. That the mental image of her in his office wasn't burned into his memory to haunt him forever.

Just now, when Jessica had been standing with him, and back at the house when he'd touched her hand, both times there was a pull so great that he'd almost given in to it. *Almost.* She wasn't only Jock's granddaughter, she was a woman with her own set of problems, her own web of issues that she needed to work through, and she deserved better than him, too. And he hadn't told her the truth about his ring. He'd purposely worn it all this time to avoid women, so he could pretend he was married and avoid the reality of being single. Of having to explain anything.

What he needed was to stay on track, deal with everything, before even thinking of letting someone else close. Even if he was in the company of a woman who was so tempting she was...*forbidden*. He needed to think of her as forbidden, and then he wouldn't be tempted. He could help her with finding the rat who'd stolen her inheritance, enjoy her company for a while, but that was it. Before long he'd be on a plane back to London to pick up the pieces of his old life and somehow try to redefine that particular puzzle so he didn't get sucked straight back into his former existence.

He dropped his forearms onto the rail of the yard and watched the horses walk slowly across the field. He picked out Patch straightaway, standing tall and surrounded by a group of mares. Seeing the old gelding made him smile. If someone had told him a few years ago he'd have learned to horseback-ride and be living on a farm in New Zealand, he'd have laughed himself stupid, but now? Now he couldn't think of anything worse than leaving it all behind, especially the old horse he'd become so attached to.

Nathan shut his eyes and breathed deep, listening to the native birdsong that had once sounded so foreign to him. It was so familiar now that he could whistle the tunes straight back to the bellbirds—they woke him just after day break with their peaceful melody. Or more often than not he was already awake, unable to sleep, preferring to be conscious so he could keep pushing the memories to the back of his mind.

He pushed back off the railing and unhitched his boot, taking one last look at the horse before walking away. Sometimes he thought about never going back, just staying here and remaining an anonymous foreigner living in the country. There was nothing he couldn't replace about his old life, even if there was a lot he felt guilty about, but he couldn't hide forever.

Nathan kept whistling back to the bellbirds as he headed for home—it was the only way he could stop himself from thinking about Jessica. And how much he wished he'd just pushed past whatever was holding him back and crushed that pouty mouth of hers against his.

CHAPTER FOUR

THE ROOM WAS starting to fill with light and Jessica shut her eyes, trying to block it out. She'd been awake since early morning, had listened to the birds slowly start to sing, and she was exhausted. Her eyes felt as if they were on fire, burning when she opened them, but it was infuriating trying to keep them shut because she knew she'd never find sleep, not after she'd been awake so long. What she needed was another five hours of shut-eye, or an entire day, even.

She kicked the covers off and stretched her legs, then sat up on the edge of her bed. If the birds hadn't been chirping, the house would have been painfully silent, just like it had been every night since she'd been home.

Jessica stood, pushed the blinds back and stared down over the fields. There were horses on the land that had been there for years, broodmares her grandfather had loved, his old horse, and a handful of young sport horses he'd been excited about finding riders for. One he'd even thought was special enough for her to campaign in Europe. But that was all over now. Even if she sold the youngster, it still wouldn't cover the full cost of bringing Teddy back.

She balled both of her hands into fists, nails digging into her palms so hard it hurt. The only consolation was that it stopped her thinking about the pain in her back that had niggled her every time she'd turned in the night—punishment for riding when she was supposed to be resting.

Jessica took a deep breath, blew it out and did it again. Her physiotherapist had told her that looking after her body was as much about looking after her entire well-being than just her physical strength, but dealing with so much loss was making it impossible for her to cope with what had happened. If she'd still been in the saddle, still been competing, then maybe she could have dealt with losing her granddad and the possible fraud with the lawyer, but right now she had nothing. *Except the farm.* And that was about to be taken from her, too.

A movement caught her eye, and she looked across toward the cottage. She smiled when she saw a little black cat, making a mental note to add cat food to her shopping list. There was always the odd wild cat around, and since she'd been a girl she'd made sure to put food out for any animal she thought might not have a home.

And then she saw Nathan. Her breathing slowed and she touched her forehead to the cool of the glass as she watched him. There was something wrong about staring at another human being without their knowledge, as if she was spying on him, but she couldn't look away. His chest was bare, his skin a lighter shade on his torso and belly as he stretched his arms above his head and stood on the porch. He was wearing shorts and nothing else, and she wondered if he'd slept in them or if he was about to go out for a run. Either way, she liked the view. His body was trim, his arms muscled, and the way he ran his hand through his hair…she gulped. She could just imagine him running his fingers through her hair, down her back, his hands firm on *her* skin.

Jessica stepped back from the window and shook her head. *Enough.* The last thing she needed was to complicate her life with a relationship, especially with everything else that she was dealing with, but it was impossible to look at Nathan and not think about him in that way. About what it would be like to be in his bed, at his side, this time of the morning.

Her phone rang, the shrill noise piercing the air and jolting her from her daydream. Jessica walked quickly down the hall and picked it up.

"Hello."

"Morning. All set for the market?"

Nathan. She hoped he hadn't seen her watching, that he didn't know she'd been admiring his half-naked body when he'd thought he was stretching in private.

"We never did decide what time we were going," she managed, shutting her eyes then popping them straight open again to get rid of the image of his chest in her mind.

"I was thinking soon. Get there before all the good produce goes."

"They have real coffee, right? You weren't just saying that the other day to get me to go?"

He laughed, a deep, throaty rumble down the line. "Yeah, but how about I make you one for the ride there? I have a stash of take-out cups handy."

"Sounds perfect," she replied. And so did he. She just had to keep reminding herself that she wasn't available for a relationship. Although if he just wanted some no-strings-attached fun...

"I'll come by in half an hour," he told her.

She hung up, dropped the phone on the bed and sprinted for the shower—she could eat breakfast there. She might not be able to ride, she might not have her granddad, but she could make an effort to make Nathan notice her. At least being around him was one thing that made her smile right now. And if he attempted to kiss her again... A slow shiver ran down her spine. Then so be it.

Nathan was pleased he had to concentrate on driving, because if he'd found Jessica distracting before, now it was virtually impossible to keep his eyes off her. She was staring out the window, oblivious to the effect she was having on him—he couldn't stop glancing at her bare thighs so close to where his hand was resting, her skin lightly tanned, her legs long and toned.

He swallowed and gripped the steering wheel tighter with the one hand he had on it. *Seriously.* It was as if he were a teenage boy lusting after a girl for the first time. He usually had way better self-control, although usually he had work to focus almost every hour of his life on. Here, there wasn't much else he could throw himself into, which was making it very hard to ignore how attracted he was to Jessica.

"Is that it there?"

Her question jolted him from his thoughts. "Yeah, that's it. I can't believe you've never been."

She turned in her seat, her body facing his now. "I was gone way longer than I expected."

"I think the market's been running for a few years, but they've become the trendy thing to do, so it's pretty popular."

She laughed. "I didn't realize so many people around here would go."

"Not from around here," he said, glancing across and catching her eye. He looked back at the road just as fast, not wanting to stray into dangerous territory. "Most of these cars only come near a country road for market day. Town people buying their organic veggies and free-range eggs, letting the kids take a ride on a pony for an exorbitant amount of money, that type of thing."

He grinned when she started to laugh even harder. "Are you serious?"

"Deadly."

"Then what the hell are *we* doing going there?" she asked.

He winked at her then inwardly cringed, wishing he hadn't done something so cheesy. "Because those town folk are on to something," he said in a stupidly executed hick accent.

Nathan noticed Jessica sink back a little into the

seat, her body language relaxed as she went back to staring out the window. He was certain she had no idea how beautiful she was. There was nothing fake or over the top about her beauty—she was just a genuinely attractive girl with big brown eyes, thick blond hair and a smile that could make a guy do anything she asked. *Or at least it could make him do anything.* And up until he'd met her, that wasn't something he thought he'd ever feel about a woman again.

"You know, it's been a long time since I've laughed like this," she said.

It had been a long time since he'd laughed and relaxed with a woman, too. If he was true with himself, it seemed like a lifetime ago; and he felt like a different man to the person he was back in London, no matter how much he might miss that life sometimes.

"Jock always said that I had to meet his amazing granddaughter," Nathan told her. "But I didn't expect the old man to go and die just so we could have dinner together."

She made a weird noise like laughter, but it quickly turned into a short sob that had her wiping at her eyes with the back of her hand. She was smiling but she was still looking out the window, clearly not wanting to meet his gaze.

"Too soon for jokes about him," he said, wishing he could kick himself for being such an idiot. He had no idea how the hell he'd gone from all messed up to trying to make stupid jokes so quickly. "I'm sorry, that was—"

"—good," she said, interrupting him. "Joking is good. It just kind of took me by surprise, that's all."

Nathan nodded at her. The last thing he'd meant to do was upset her—he knew better than anyone how hard it was to deal with loss, to move on. He took a deep, shaky breath and gripped the wheel a little harder with his right hand. He seriously needed to get a grip.

"When I lost my wife, I didn't think I'd ever…" He grimaced, the words almost impossible to expel; his chest was tightening, constricting, from his trying to talk about what had happened. He wanted to let her in so she would know that he wasn't lying when he said he understood, but it was harder than tough. It was almost impossible.

Jessica was still staring out the window, unable to face him or maybe finding it too hard to accept what they'd been talking about, trying to keep her emotions in check. But she did reach for his hand, her fingers searching out his and squeezing.

The contact gave him the prompt he needed to continue, wanting to reach out to her. Nathan fought the choke in his throat—he'd tried to talk to friends, then a therapist, and yet the closest he'd ever come to opening up was with Jock during the hours they'd spent talking. Now he was almost ready to confide in the old man's granddaughter. *Almost.*

"Jessica, my wife, she…" He shook his head, hating what he was about to say, changing his mind at the last minute, not wanting to see the look on her face if she knew the truth. Because it was his fault— he blamed himself and he always would. And since he'd been in New Zealand he hadn't spoken about it once, hadn't told anyone, because he was ashamed and it was easier hiding from the truth.

Now Jessica's fingers were interlocked with his and she'd finally angled her body more toward him. He was glad he was driving, because it meant he didn't have to look at her as he spoke.

"The way she died was pretty traumatic," he finally said, stopping short of telling her that she'd committed suicide in their own home. He just couldn't get the words out. What would Jessica think of him if she knew the truth? "So when I tell you I understand what you're going through, that you can talk to me and I'll get it, I'm telling the truth." It was a cop-out and he was angry with himself, but he was also scared of losing whatever connection he had with Jessica. Of talking about what happened with someone who didn't already know. "I know what it's like to have no one to open up to."

The car was silent, the only noise the rumble as they turned off the main road onto a gravel one, slowly heading into the entrance of the property where the market was held.

"So that's why you're here," she said, her voice soft, almost a whisper, as if she were thinking out aloud. "It wasn't just the heart attack that sent you packing."

He didn't say anything. There was nothing to say, not when he didn't want to tell her any more of the story.

"You needed to get away from everything, including the wife you'd lost."

She moved her fingers across his, loosening her grasp on them as she touched him. It was an unfamiliar sensation to him now, the soft, gentle touch of a woman—the way his wife used to touch him, before they'd slowly, painfully become like strangers.

"She was an artist, well known," he told her, "and I didn't handle being in the public eye so well. She thrived on it, in the beginning, anyway."

Jessica's touch was firmer now, as if she was trying to comfort him rather than fire the flames of whatever attraction existed between them. "So you needed some time. Understandable."

He pulled over when they were close to the market. "I have to go back soon, but right now this is where I want to be."

Their eyes locked, her expression impossible to read. Was it stupid to think that where he wanted to be was right here with her? A woman he hadn't even truly known a few days ago? Maybe he'd just become lonely here without people around him, especially since Jock had passed away, although the way he was feeling about Jessica seemed a whole lot more about being attracted to her than just loneliness.

Jessica patted his hand one last time, before unclipping her seat belt as he pulled over behind a line of other cars. He watched as she tucked her long hair behind her ears and smiled across at him; his eyes were drawn to her lips, her full mouth as the corners tipped up. It was so easy to forget everything else when he was with her, at least for the moments when she was looking back at him.

"Sounds like we both need to be distracted from reality," she said. "What do you say we drink coffee and forget about everything for a morning?"

He pushed open his door, needing to get out of the car and away from being so closely confined with Jessica. He didn't trust himself not to just lean over and kiss the words from her mouth.

"How about we make it coffee and pastry?" he suggested, locking the car once she'd stepped out and being careful not to walk too close to her. "The pain au chocolat is seriously good."

"So much for healthy food, huh?" she said jokingly, nudging him in the side with her elbow and moving way too close for comfort.

He resisted the unfamiliar urge to loop his arm around her waist and draw her closer. It was weird how comfortable he already felt with her—comfortable in some ways and completely out of his depth in others. "A guy has to have a treat every once in a while."

Jessica cast a quick glance sideways at him before her eyes darted away again. She was as hesitant as he was, which meant they were doing a kind of dance around one another, waiting for something to happen that might not if he didn't just…what?

Man up and bloody well kiss her, that was what. Only right now it was a hell of a lot easier to say than do.

Jessica stopped at the stall selling pastries, her nose filling with the delicious aroma of pastry, fruit and chocolate. The only thing that came close to making her taste buds so happy was the cappuccino she was already sipping.

"So this is breakfast, huh?" she asked.

Nathan leaned over her shoulder, so close she could smell his aftershave. If she moved a tiny bit to the right she'd be able to touch her cheek to his, feel if he had a hint of stubble already on his jaw, but instead she stayed dead still and stared at the food in front of them.

"Morning!"

A friendly voice sung out at the same time as a woman appeared.

"Good morning," Nathan replied, pointing to the pains au chocolat they had been salivating over. "Make it four this morning."

Jessica laughed. "Four? They're massive."

His mouth was dangerously close to hers when he turned, grinning. "Yeah, but they're so good that I usually get a second coffee and eat another on the drive home."

The woman beamed at them as she handed over two paper bags. "You two make such a gorgeous couple. I can't believe you've never brought your wife here with you before."

It took Jessica a moment to process what the woman had just said, and when she did she looked at Nathan, wide-eyed. She was sure he'd be as surprised as her.

"Oh no, we're not—" Nathan tried to say.

"I mean, he's always wearing a ring, so I knew he had a wife, but you're even more gorgeous than I expected."

Nathan cleared his throat, loudly, and Jessica just made some kind of a grunt in her throat before taking the bags and numbly nodding.

"Thank you," she mumbled.

"You're welcome. Come anytime!"

Jessica nudged Nathan with her elbow, hating the awkward silence between them and not knowing what else to do. She hardly knew what to say!

"Well that was weird."

He shot her a funny sideways look that turned into a smile. "Sorry. The one day I don't wear my ring and someone goes and thinks you're—"

"—your wife," she finished for him. "At least she thought we looked *gorgeous together.*"

Nathan gestured for her to sit on the grass, then bent down himself, put his coffee cup on the ground and opened his brown paper bag.

"I think she said *you* were gorgeous," he mumbled. "And it was worth it for how good these will taste."

Jessica followed his lead and took a bite, raising her eyebrows as she did so. *Wow.* "Okay, so for the second time in as many days you've managed to give me something incredible to eat. Amazing."

Nathan's eyes left hers and dropped to her mouth. She watched him, held her breath as he silently stared.

"You have a little something…" He put down his bag and leaned forward, brushing his thumb against the side of her mouth.

She started to reply, to wipe it away herself, but when Nathan's skin met hers everything else stopped. Jessica stayed impossibly still, her breathing becoming shallow when he tipped even further toward her. She licked her coffee-and-pastry-sweet lips, and when Nathan's gaze drifted to her eyes again, made it clear what he was thinking, she decided not to hold back.

Suddenly it was as if there was no one else in the world except them, as if the crowd gathered at the market had disappeared. Nathan closed the distance between them before she had time to overthink what was happening, his mouth barely touching hers for a split second, giving her the chance to pull away then tentatively touching hers. Jessica was still holding her coffee in one hand, the other propping up the weight of her body; the only part of her moving was her lips. She matched the gentleness of Nathan's kiss, a little sigh escaping her lips when he pulled back, pausing before kissing her again. Only this time it was less gentle, his mouth firmer against hers as their tongues collided.

Nathan stroked her shoulder as they kissed, his thumb moving back and forward in a gentle massage. And it wasn't until he slowly took his lips off hers that she came back to reality—heard the squeals of children and noticed how many other people were bustling around them.

She looked up at him, into his rich brown eyes that now seemed even darker, more intense, than she'd ever seen them. But what she saw took her by surprise; there was conflict in his gaze. A flicker from happiness to concern, maybe regret, and right then in that moment she wanted to do whatever it took to wipe that edge of uncertainty away.

"Hey," she said, leaning in closer again, never breaking their eye contact.

"Hey back," he replied, propping his arm behind hers so he was leaning closer to her as he supported his weight, his expression more relaxed instead of looking as if he was about to bolt.

Even though she'd fantasized about him all morning after she'd seen him half naked, the kiss had still been unexpected. *Unexpected but definitely not unwanted.* And his hesitation had been kind of unexpected, too, although given that he'd lost a wife she didn't know why she should have expected anything different.

"So, ah, I hope that's not going to make things awkward between us," he finally said.

Jessica laughed at the husky tone of his voice. He was so close to her, her head tilted back to look up at him, that she could have kissed him without having to do anymore than lean a little. *And she decided to do exactly that, to show him how she felt.*

She raised her chin and looked up at Nathan, stretching up and catching his lips against hers. She abandoned her coffee cup and draped her arm around Nathan's neck instead, her hand cupping just under the base of his skull. When she let her mouth slide off his, she stared straight into his eyes again as she spoke.

"Definitely not awkward," she murmured. "But a whole lot more interesting."

His laugh was soft, as was the kiss he dropped to

her lips before closing his arm around her shoulder and drawing her close.

"How have I managed to stay out of trouble this entire trip, and now here I am kissing a girl at a market?" His tone was relaxed now, the worry lines that had bracketed his eyes as good as gone.

Jessica shook her head. "No idea. I'm supposed to be miserable, mourning and convalescing, so this definitely wasn't part of my plan."

"Oh, so this is all my fault?" he asked, leaning dangerously close to her again. His morning stubble tickled her cheek, brushing just hard enough against her to make her feel it.

"Definitely your fault. You're the one who suggested the pastries, so you can take all the blame."

Jess reached for her coffee again and took a sip, as much to avoid the full intensity of Nathan's stare as anything else. She might have sounded confident sparring with him like that, but her stomach was starting to flip like a pancake now that he was slowly coming out of his shell. Nathan was gorgeous and charming, so there wasn't a part of her that didn't want to be in his arms. Her problem with men was in the long term, even though logically she knew that wasn't going to be an issue with Nathan. He'd already told her that he wouldn't even be in the country much longer, so what harm was there in having a little fun?

"Want to take a look around the rest of the market?" he asked, sitting up straighter and finishing the last of his coffee.

"Sure. Maybe we could buy some food to stop my pantry from looking like no one lives in the house."

"And maybe we could buy some ingredients so we can cook dinner together tonight?"

Jessica took his hand when he held it out and stood, unable to stop smiling when they walked off hand in hand. There'd been a spark between them before, but now there was a pull so strong, sending flushes through her entire body, that she knew there was no way she could say no to him even if she wanted to. Something had changed between them, and she liked it.

He shouldn't have done it. No matter how incredible it had been kissing Jessica, after thinking of doing little else for the past two days, it had been stupid. He should have gone with his instincts and kept his hands and his mind off her—or maybe it had been his instincts that were getting him in trouble.

He was renting her guest house. She was Jock's granddaughter. She was…he ran his hands through his hair, pleased they were walking so she didn't notice his agitation. *She was a beautiful woman.* That was the truth of it, and nothing about that was going to change anytime soon. And he was in no shape to enter any kind of relationship.

"Look at these," he heard Jessica say.

He stopped when she tugged him back to a stall.

"Gourmet meals to take home," she said, glancing at him as she spoke. "The chicken lasagna looks amazing."

Nathan ran a hand down her back, fighting the feelings of guilt at touching her, her body warm to the touch even through her T-shirt. It had been a long time since he'd felt like this, not since he'd first met his wife—the thrill of every bump and touch of another human being—and it was so foreign to him that it was intoxicating. Was worth being outside of his comfort zone.

"Sounds like a much better way to impress you than trying to cook something from scratch."

Her smile caught him like an animal in the glare of a headlight. There was something about Jessica that changed his mood when he was around her.

"Let's not stop there, then," she said with an easy laugh. "How about we go back to the cupcake stand and take a few of those home for dessert, too?"

Right now he would have said yes to anything she wanted if it meant keeping that beautiful smile beaming in his direction and his mind off everything else.

"Anything you want," he said, nodding to the stall owner who was hovering over the lasagna.

"Anything?" she asked.

He raised an eyebrow and took a quick survey of the market. "Anything," he affirmed. "The worst you can do is go crazy on food, right?"

So much for his vow to stay single after his wife had died, to never let himself get close to another woman again. Everything had been going so perfectly to plan, and then Jessica had appeared and crushed all his best intentions as if they'd never even existed. He should have told her about Marie when he'd had the chance before, but the truth was he wasn't even going to be in the country for much longer. Why tell her something that could change the way she thought about him when he could just keep it to himself and enjoy Jessica's company? So long as she knew he was here for only a short time, that was all that mattered. He couldn't commit to anything more than a fling at best, no matter how he felt about her.

And the less he thought about his past, the better he was starting to feel about his future.

CHAPTER FIVE

Even if she'd wanted to, Jessica couldn't stop smiling. There were plenty of things that should have stopped her—the pain shooting intermittently through her back and the prospect of losing her farm for starters —but a certain someone was making her body hum like it hadn't in a long time. *And that certain someone had arrived.*

As the sound of his knock at the back door echoed through the living room, she took a sip of wine for confidence, then spun around to find Nathan less than twenty feet away.

"Sorry, should I have waited?"

She shook her head. "No."

"Jock always had the door open, and I was used to wandering on in whenever I was passing."

She opened the fridge and retrieved a beer for him. "I still find it hard to comprehend that you knew him so well. I mean, it's kind of weird but also kind of amazing at the same time."

Nathan took the beer bottle and clinked it against hers before taking a sip. There was still a flicker of something, a hint that he wasn't quite as relaxed in her company as he appeared. The nervous way he picked at the label of the bottle, the way he glanced away if they held eye contact for too long.

"Talking about Jock," he said, taking a few steps back and sitting on the edge of the table, his concern obvious. "Do you think he'd be okay with what happened today? Between us?"

Jessica liked the fact that he thought so highly of her granddad. "The one guy he warned me about turned out to be a jackass, but I'm guessing he wouldn't have steered me away from you. Not if he liked you enough to spend so much time with you."

She watched as he swilled back a whole lot more beer. Something was definitely on his mind.

"Want to talk about him?" he asked.

Jessica sighed. "Not really. All you need to know is that he was engaged to another woman, and I had no idea."

Nathan almost choked on his beer. "You're kidding me?"

She shook her head. "'fraid not."

"I really like you, and I would never lie to you like that," he said, face serious as he spoke and making her almost drop her wineglass. "But I need to be honest before—"

"—we eat our amazing lasagna?" she attempted to joke.

He smiled but his expression was still serious. "Jess, I have to head back to London sooner than I thought. Probably in a week's time," he said with a grimace. "I've had this rule that I only turn on my phone once a week, clear my messages and let my assistant run through anything urgent with me, and it's kind of backfired. I just checked them before I came over—that's why I'm late."

She laughed, but it didn't sound natural. How could he need to leave when she'd only just met him? She'd known it wasn't going to turn into anything serious between them, but a week?

"I'm not sure whether I'm more shocked that you're leaving so soon, or that you only turn your phone on once a week."

He pushed off the table and reached for her hand— it was an unexpected gesture that made her wish she had longer with him.

"I've been here for months, and suddenly I meet you and have to leave," he said. "Ironic, but true."

There was something so easy between them, but at the same time the attraction was enough to make her blood feel like it was on fire, bubbling through her veins at his touch.

"So it's just me and you for a week, huh?" she asked, letting go of his hand and touching his jawline. The stubble was gone, replaced with skin that was impossibly soft.

"A week," he replied.

They stared at each other, neither moving for what seemed like a lifetime. Jessica could hear the exhale of her breath, every one of her senses aware—the aroma of Nathan's cologne, the cool of the glass against her hand, the thud of her own heart as she waited...*for what?*

Nathan reached for her glass, his eyes never leaving hers even as he took it from her and set it down on the counter behind her. Jessica stayed immobile, becoming breathless as he slid his hand down her back, stopping when he reached the curve just above her bottom to pull her body hard against his.

"What do you say we make the most of this week?"

The husky, lethal tone of his voice would have melted her to a puddle at his feet if he hadn't been holding on to her. Gone was any uncertainty, replaced with a desire she could see shining from his eyes.

"I say…" she began, but she didn't bother finishing her sentence, standing on tiptoe to show him with her mouth instead.

His mouth was hot and wet as he kissed her back; his arms were still around her as he pulled her forward and against himself again. All thoughts disappeared from her mind as she let her tongue explore Nathan's mouth, running her fingers through his hair, her other hand sliding across his broad, muscular shoulders. She wanted Nathan, there was no hint of a doubt in her mind, and the fact that he was only here for another week…*it was perfect.* Long-term relationships terrified her, and so did one-night stands usually, but this was different.

"Jessica." Nathan's voice was a whisper across her lips.

"Mmm," she managed back, tugging at his hair to try to get him to kiss her again, and nipping at his lower lip when he didn't comply.

"I don't want you to get the wrong idea," he mumbled, as she tried to distract him with her mouth. "This can only be—"

This time she managed to silence him, and he didn't bother trying to finish his sentence. Jessica sighed against his mouth, and for the first time in what seemed like forever, she forgot about everything else going on in her life and just enjoyed the moment.

So much for staying out of trouble. There was something about Jessica that had made him forget everything except for how much he wanted her in his arms. And there was also something about her that was helping him put his painful past in a compartment of his mind.

"You," he whispered in her ear, "are so beautiful."

She turned her face slightly so he was looking straight at her, her long lashes hiding her eyes when she glanced down. He didn't give her the chance to change her mind or become shy, dropping his mouth to hers in a kiss that had him fighting to hold himself back. Jessica's fingers dug into his shoulder, fisting a handful of his T-shirt as their lips moved back and forth, holding on to him like she didn't want him to escape.

Nathan tried to keep things slow, wanting to enjoy every second of Jessica against him, but he couldn't hold back. When she slipped a hand under the front of his top, her smooth palm exploring his torso and then running up his chest, he was a goner. He scooped her up, both hands on her bottom to support her weight, groaning when she locked her legs around his waist.

Nathan walked forward a few steps until her back was against the wall, taking her weight in one hand, the other palm pushing flat against the wall above her head. He dipped his mouth to her neck as she moaned for more, lips quickly finding hers again, his hand dropping almost as fast as it had risen to push up the hem of her top, sliding across her smooth skin. He wanted to touch every part of her, to lose himself in her arms, and he wanted it now.

"The bedroom," she gasped against his cheek when she pushed him back.

Nathan didn't need to be asked twice, and he didn't give a hoot about where they were, so long as she didn't want to stop. He kept her in his arms, easily carrying her, walking through the living room and trying to kiss her at the same time.

"This way?"

She nodded, nuzzling his neck and pressing such soft kisses there he could hardly stand it. "Uh-huh." Her tongue traced a line almost to his ear before trailing back down again, then she sucked, laughing when he protested.

"You," he said, stopping at the stairs and bending forward to drop her on one of them, "are wicked."

She laughed and arched her back. "Ahhh." Her smile turned into a frown filled with pain as her body twisted to the side.

"What happened? Your back?" Nathan didn't know what to do other than hover over her.

"It'll be fine," she said, but he could tell she was still sore. "One minute it can be fine, just a noticeable ache, and the next I get a shooting pain that sends me through the roof."

"Would a massage help?" he asked, leaning over her and kissing the frown away.

"Maybe," she replied, the pain starting to disappear from her face, eyes softening again.

"Then how about I carry you to your room and rub the pain away?" he suggested, carefully scooping her back up in his arms and carrying her up the stairs.

Instead of her legs wrapped around him, this time she had her head against his chest while he carried her. "Sounds heavenly," she murmured.

What was heavenly were the soft tendrils of her hair brushing his face, the faint scent of perfume, the weight of her in his arms. And if he had to go slow and massage her, then that was exactly what he'd do.

"In there," she said when they got to the top, her arms locked around his neck.

Nathan kicked open the door so they could enter, stopping only when he got to her bed. He lowered her onto her side, not wanting to put her on her back again in case he hurt her.

"I'm not going to break," she said, looking up at him.

He smiled. "So you'd rather I was rough?"

Her grin made him laugh. "Just forget about my back," she ordered. "I'll tell you if it hurts."

Nathan shrugged, kicking off his boots and pushing her over so she was on her stomach. "Once I've massaged you," he said, "then I'll forget about your back."

He brushed aside her long hair and gently started to massage her shoulders.

"Mmmm."

Her moan was encouraging. Nathan ran his fingers down her back a little further, spreading out his palms so he could knead with his thumbs, fingers edging out toward her sides. He kept going, inching down her back, listening to the soft noises she was making. When she stiffened a little he stopped, not wanting to put pressure on somewhere that hurt her, but as soon as he did she mumbled to keep going. So he did exactly that.

Only the longer he had his hands on her the faster his resolve to take things slow started to disappear.

Jessica turned, pushing Nathan back slightly as she did so. His gaze held a question that she was only too happy to answer. She cupped the back of his head and brought his face down to hers, kissing him slowly at first. He complied—it was she who wanted more, who couldn't keep the painfully slow pace.

"You liked that?" he asked in a husky voice. "Because there's plenty more where that came from."

CHAPTER SIX

IT HAD BEEN a long time since Jessica had woken with a smile on her face. Usually the second she opened her eyes everything came crashing back to her—the accident, the pain and her granddad. This morning was different. Sunlight warmed her bare arm, and the rest of her was heated by Nathan's warm body pressed against hers. The weight was comforting, even though she was used to having her bed to herself, and when she turned slowly to make sure she stayed in his arms, she was able to indulge in surveying his face. His nose was straight, dark eyebrows and lashes the perfect outline for his chocolate eyes when they were open. There were faint lines around his eyes and a light laugh line bracketing his mouth, but otherwise his strong face was flawless.

"Good morning," he mumbled, eyes opening slowly after he spoke.

"Morning," she replied, leaning in to brush a kiss across his lips.

Nathan kissed her back, but it was a lazy kind of kiss—nothing like the night before but every bit as enjoyable.

"I've been thinking," he said, breaking contact only to speak, his mouth searching out hers again.

"While you were sleeping?" she murmured.

He chuckled and stroked her cheek, brushing hair from her face as it fell across her eye. "Before I fell asleep actually, and then again the moment I woke up and saw your face. Which is unusual for me, because usually I lie awake half the night and do nothing but think because I can't sleep."

She liked that he'd slept well with her beside him, and it had been the same for her. Being asleep in Nathan's arms had been so comforting, made her feel so safe, that she'd slept peacefully right through the night, too.

"There's something about being with you," he said, "something that's made me, hell, I don't know."

"What?" she asked, even though she felt the same. That there was something about being with him that had made her relax, made her believe that she would get past everything that had happened.

"I guess I just feel like I can talk to you," he said, his fingers twirling a strand of her hair. "Like I can just be me, and I haven't felt like that in a long time."

She relaxed against him. "I know what you mean." It was as if they were two lost souls, the losses they'd both suffered drawing them together, and each somehow understood a little of what the other had been through.

"This is going to sound crazy, but that thinking I was doing overnight? Well, there's something I want to ask you."

Her heart started to beat a little too fast, just as it had the night before when he'd first kissed her. *He'd been thinking about something to do with her?* "What is it?"

"Come with me."

His words were a simple statement but they held as much power as if he'd just delivered a presidential speech.

"Come with you?" She wasn't sure exactly what he meant, what he was asking her.

"To London," he said, stroking down her arm and catching her hand, linking their fingers. "You can fly back with me, see Teddy, have a holiday."

She took a shaky breath, forcing herself to stay still. Her instincts when it came to men were to flee, because she knew how easy words were to say and how easier promises were to break. *He actually wanted her to go with him to London?*

"I don't know what to say." It was the truth—she had no idea what she even wanted to tell him.

"Then just say yes," he said, leaning in to kiss her jaw before making a trail down her neck and to her collarbone. "I'm not ready to say goodbye to you yet. It's a win-win situation."

"For who?"

His throaty laugh sent a shiver through her body.

"Both of us. I want to see more of you, and this is the only way that's going to happen," he said.

"So we'd extend our fun for another week or so?" Jessica asked.

"Uh-huh. What do you say?" He looked at her,

waiting for an answer. "I have to book my flights later today."

What she really wanted was for him to go back to kissing her, to lie in his arms and think about nothing else for the rest of the day. Or the week.

"Yes," she said, not sure if it was the right thing to say when she'd only just got back and had so much going on. Then again, the distraction would be kind of nice, so long as she had enough money in the bank to keep someone on to feed the horses and keep an eye on everything for her.

"Great," Nathan said, taking her mind off her worries again as he stroked her shoulder. "I'll get my assistant to book us first-class tickets today."

Jessica sighed as he kept up the stroking, his fingers like silk as they drifted across her skin. There was something dangerous about spending time with Nathan—she didn't want to get used to luxuries like first class, not when she couldn't even afford to send her horse back via ship, and having a man like Nathan around…he was kind, gorgeous and fun, and that wasn't something she wanted to become accustomed to, either.

He brushed his mouth over hers, his hand to the small of her back. She might not want to get used to this, but it sure was fun for now.

"So what are we going to do today?" Nathan asked Jessica as he came up behind her and looped his arms around her waist, nudging aside her hair so he could nuzzle her neck.

She twisted in his embrace and kissed him, casually dropping her arms over his shoulders. It was weird to be so relaxed with him, to be touching him so openly after they'd danced around their attraction in the beginning.

"Maybe we could take the horses out?" she said.

"Or maybe I could go over some of your granddad's paperwork with you? Take a look with fresh eyes in case you've missed something?"

She groaned. "Or maybe we could just go back to bed?"

He dropped a kiss to her forehead. "I'm tempted, but I also want to help you get to the bottom of this before we go."

This time her groan was even louder, but she pushed off him and leaned back against the counter. "How about I show you where to look and leave you to it for half an hour?" she asked. "I've gone just about cross-eyed trying to sift through everything, but I'd love you to take a look."

Nathan followed her, planting his hands on the counter on either side of her and leaning in for one last kiss, moving his lips slowly back and forth across hers.

"I'm going to call in a favor from an old friend, see if he can help," Nathan said, knowing that she'd probably protest if he told her he was going to spend money on a private investigator to get to the bottom of the issue. "There's no way anyone's going to force you into selling this place, not if I have anything to do with it."

Jessica's smile told him he was doing the right thing. He took her hand when she offered it, and she led him to Jock's office. The room was immaculate, just like it had been when the old man was alive, and he followed her to the desk at the far end of the library-like space. There were a few piles of paper and Post-it notes stuck over everything.

"I have this sneaking suspicion that some of the properties have been sold either without my grandfather knowing somehow, or at a huge loss. I can't figure it out completely, but I feel like I'm on the right trail."

Nathan let go of her hand and moved behind the desk, scanning the piles and nodding as he listened to her. "We need to find the deeds, make a list of who else he used for business. His accountant, any other professional advisors."

"Sounds like a plan. You take a look over everything, I'll take a shower, then we can sit down and work through it all."

Nathan dropped into the big chair and ran his hand across one of the paper piles, then reached for a pen. It had been a long time since he'd sat down to work in this type of environment, and he felt an almost forgotten type of buzz at actually taking on a task. He'd had a great time doing nothing for a while, but there was a part of him desperate for a purpose again, for a challenge that only work could bring, and he knew he was doing the right thing heading home.

"Nathan?"

He looked up.

"Thank you," she said. "I don't find it easy to trust sometimes, but I feel like, I don't know, that we've kind of told each other everything. That we can count on each other."

He refused to let his smile fade until she'd left the room, and then it dropped into a frown. *He'd told her a lot, but he hadn't told her everything.*

Jessica stretched and tried to ignore the twinge in her back. She needed to head outside for a walk and do her exercises, but she had this feeling they were about to figure something out. That they were so close to realizing what had gone wrong with Jock's affairs, that the answer was right under their noses and they were missing it each time they came close.

"Do you know what I think?"

She dropped the time line she'd been studying and drew her knees up to her chin, sitting on the floor. "What?" Her eyes were stinging from staring at the tiny words from all the legal documents she'd gone over, and her back was seriously starting to ache.

"I think your grandfather agreed to sell the individual properties, but what he signed or agreed to aren't the transactions we see in front of us."

Jessica crossed her arms, listening carefully to Nathan. "I don't know that I'm following you."

He stood and walked slowly over to the window. She watched as he stared out, as if he was still processing the whole thing in his mind.

"Let's say that he believed there was a willing buyer at a certain price." Nathan turned around and ran a hand through his hair, a gesture she'd started to notice that he did a lot. "Jock signed the sale and purchase agreement, in front of his lawyer, who has then fraudulently forged the rest of the paperwork at a different price to a completely different buyer, because there was no genuine one to start with."

She shook her head. "You don't think that's too far-fetched?" It wasn't that she didn't think it could have happened, but for it to have happened to her granddad was kind of hard to get her head around.

"I just don't see how else it could have happened, because from what I see here Jock intended on making the sales. Maybe he wanted to free up some money because he knew he was…"

Jessica froze, the tone of Nathan's voice and the way he'd just stopped talking sending alarm bells off in her head. "He knew he was what?"

His face remained impassive, not even a flicker of change, as if he was trying to pretend he hadn't just said what he had. But she knew he was keeping something back, something she needed to know.

"Nathan?" She said again, "He knew he was what?"

He blew out an audible breath, leaning back against the windowsill. "Because he knew he was dying," he said in a soft voice.

Jessica's hands started to tremble and she folded them on her lap, trying to stay calm. "You're telling me that he knew something was wrong? That he was sick?" *Surely her granddad would have told her, would have given her the chance to come home and seen him before he passed.*

Nathan nodded, crossed the room and dropped to the carpet beside her. "Yes."

He took both of her hands in his and stared into her eyes, his expression so full of concern that it made it hard for her to hold back her emotion. She didn't want to believe him, but she knew deep down that he was telling the truth. This man who had been so kind to her, who had helped her heal in a way she could hardly comprehend, would never lie to her. They'd shared a lot and she trusted him so much it scared her.

She sat up straighter, even though it hurt. The easy thing to do would be to yell at Nathan, take her anger and sadness out on him, but she knew it wasn't his fault. If she wanted someone to blame for not telling her the truth, it wasn't him.

"Jess?" Nathan's eyes sought out hers, his dark gaze stormy.

"How about you finish telling me your conspiracy theory?" she replied in a quiet voice. "Then we can go for a ride and you can tell me what I need to know."

Nathan nodded and let go of her hands. He stayed close, but even though his body was near she'd never felt so alone. Emotion threatened to choke her but she blocked it, tried to push the thoughts out of her head and just concentrate on what Nathan was saying.

"I don't think he could have acted alone," he told her. "For this to have worked, the lawyer must have had a buyer lined up, perhaps even a company he's involved with, and then they would have purchased it well below valuation and resold it soon after for a big profit. Or be planning to sell each property soon."

It all made sense, she had to give him that. "And because my grandfather was sick, he never realized what was going on."

"Not to mention a power of attorney putting his lawyer in a genuine position of power."

Jessica shut her eyes, taking it all in, processing what Nathan was saying. If he was right, she *had* to fight to get to the bottom of it, to save what was rightfully hers.

"So what do I do now?" she asked, standing and carefully stretching her body to limber up her back before she moved too far.

"Now you let me appoint an investigator, and we have a fun week before we pack up and head for the airport. If he's guilty he'll be prevented from ever practicing law again, and you'll be able to sue him."

She still couldn't believe she'd said yes to traveling back to London with Nathan—there was so much in her head she could hardly process it all at once.

"I can't afford an investigator," she said.

"But I can," Nathan told her, rising and standing behind her. His hands closed over her shoulders and rubbed gently. "And don't go telling me that you won't take charity," he said when she started to protest. "You can pay me back someday if you like, once it's all sorted out, but I'm doing this as much for Jock as I am for you."

As heavenly as the massage was, she forced herself to step away and turned around to face him.

"Speaking of my grandfather," she said, "how about we go for a walk and you can start on that telling-me-everything promise."

Nathan walked alongside Jessica, glancing at her every few seconds. She was beautiful. From the way her golden hair tumbled over her shoulders, the way her eyes always locked on his when she smiled, and the glimpses of skin he kept getting when she stretched—it was impossible not to think about the night they'd spent together. Just the flash of her bare stomach when she held her arms above her head before had reminded him of his mouth on that particular stretch of skin, how she'd felt in his arms.

He clamped his jaw and tried to push the memories away long enough to talk to her about her grandfather. The words had slipped out earlier, which meant he was about to break a promise to a man who'd meant so much to him. Not to mention the fact that he was shaking in his boots over the way he was behaving with Jessica, how natural it seemed to be with her.

"So tell me," Jessica said, not letting him stay silent any longer.

Nathan knew she'd be hurt that he knew something about Jock that she didn't. He reached for her, touching his hand to her lower back as they walked.

"We talked a lot, every day, and there are things I told your granddad that I'll probably never tell another soul."

Jessica glanced at him before looking straight ahead again, arms folded across her chest now.

"And he opened up to you, too?"

"Yeah," Nathan replied, not wanting to betray the old man's confidences but needing to tell her some of it. "He knew he was sick, but only for a short time, and he didn't want you to give up on your dreams when you were so close. He said it would have meant you not competing at Badminton."

She stopped moving and Nathan put his arms around her, drawing her close when he saw tears in her eyes. He wanted to comfort her, wanted to help break the pain that he knew was taking hold of her.

"The old bugger knew I'd come straight home, didn't he? And then he probably felt even worse when I had the fall."

Nathan nodded, holding her tight in his arms, his chin touching the top of her head. "He said there was nothing you could do for him, and he'd rather know you were doing what you loved. But then he regretted it, because if he had told you…"

Her body shuddered and he kissed her forehead, wrapping his arms even more firmly around her.

"I might not have had the accident."

"He was an incredible man, and he didn't want you to see him dying," Nathan told her, keeping his voice low. "But in the end it was the heart attack that killed him, not the cancer."

Jessica's arms were around him now, her head pressed to his chest like she wasn't ever going to let go or step away.

"At least he had you during those months," she mumbled, sniffing as she spoke. "At least he had you."

Yeah, he had. But the truth was that Jock had done a lot more for him than vice versa. When he'd arrived he'd been in a hell of a state—a dark vacuum that he had never thought he would be able to emerge from. And Jock had patiently waited him out, let him talk in his own time, then given him advice from the heart.

And then along had come Jessica. And for the first time in months, he'd almost found peace. Almost. Her granddad had been there for him, but it was being with Jessica that had slowly started to make him heal.

Jessica stared up at the sky, one hand held high above her head to shield her face from the bright sunshine. Today had been…*interesting.* She'd woken up in bed with Nathan, they'd talked about what might have happened to her inheritance, and she'd found out just what lengths her grandfather had been willing to go to for her. Always putting her ambitions ahead of his own.

"You never did say why, after all this time, you're having to leave in such a hurry," she said, thinking out aloud as they lay side by side.

Nathan reached for her hand, the one that was absently plucking grass, tucking his fingers over hers.

"I'm not just a banker."

The man was full of surprises. "You're not?"

"I saw an opportunity to buy into a small company

that was trying to launch a new energy drink a couple of years ago," he said, propping himself up on one elbow and looking down at her as he spoke. "I purchased the majority share, invested a crazy amount of money into the company, and we've not long ago started to distribute through North America as well as Europe. I need to go back to finalize the deal to float the company on the public stock exchange. All in all, it's been a pretty amazing investment."

She laughed. "Sorry, I don't think it's funny, I'm just kind of amazed that you're so..."

Nathan grinned. "What?"

"I don't know, you just seem so normal. But you're also this crazy successful business person."

"I am normal," he insisted, dropping a kiss to her mouth that was casual yet so unexpected that it had her pulse racing way too fast in less than a second. "Although I think I'm still hanging on to part of my childhood. I still want to prove to my father that I can do anything I want and be successful in my own right, so aside from that, yeah, I'm pretty normal."

"But you're also insanely wealthy, right?" she asked, wondering if she should have just kept that particular comment to herself. "I guess that's a good reminder to your dad."

Nathan shrugged, but she knew what that meant. He just wasn't going to brag about it even if he was proud of what he'd achieved.

"So when I'm in London, would you be offended if I head to the Cotswolds to see Teddy the day after we arrive?" she asked.

Nathan bent down low over her, his mouth barely an inch from hers. "It's the only reason you said yes to coming, isn't it?"

She tried to shake her head but he caught her mouth, his lips punishing hers. He then moved her hands above her head and pinned them there.

"It's not the only reason," she whispered back to him.

His laugh was husky. "Then how about you show me what the other reasons are?"

Jessica fought a giggle as he nipped her ear, before taking her mouth against his again, his lips impossibly soft as he grazed them back and forth over hers. There were so many things she should be doing, so many things that needed her attention. Although faced with a decision between reality and Nathan, it was impossible not to choose the latter.

A warning signal in her brain was trying to alert her again, she knew it was, but she chose to ignore it. Nathan was here for less than a week, and she was only going away with him for a short time. Which meant she couldn't get attached to him, didn't expect anything from him other than what they were doing right now. Just because her mom had pined for a man who'd broken her heart when he left didn't mean Jessica was ever going to make the same mistake. She was in charge of her own destiny, and nothing was going to change that. Not a riding accident, not a fraudulent lawyer, and certainly not a man. One bad ex didn't mean she needed to avoid all men for eternity, either.

Nathan could distract her all he wanted in the short term. That wasn't something she was ever going to say no to. Not with his mouth grazing her lips and his hands skimming against her skin. This was the kind of distraction she was only too happy to surrender to.

CHAPTER SEVEN

"I can't believe we're actually boarding this plane."

Nathan slung an arm around Jessica's shoulders. He could hardly believe it, either. After so long in New Zealand there had been times he'd thought he might never leave. Going home was something he'd dreaded, although now he was getting excited about work again. Banking, not so much. But the company was something he was passionate about, and if he left it for much longer…well, there was only so many meetings that his poor assistant could defer on his behalf. It was one part of his career that he definitely wanted to salvage.

"You know everything's going to work out while you're gone, right?" he asked.

Jessica leaned into him, her arm finding his waist. "Yeah, but even if you're right about everything, what's the best that can happen?"

"The fraud is exposed and you sue them," he said, frowning at the worried look on her face.

"And that'll take how long?" she asked with a groan. "And if they've got no accessible money, I might never get anything back and I'll lose the farm anyway."

"You won't."

"I could."

He held her closer, their bodies skimming as they walked side by side. "I won't let that happen." She might not be comfortable with him spending his money to help her, but he was, and that was what mattered. The fact that neither she nor her grandfather would have ever expected his help was what made him so determined to offer it.

"Mr. Bell, right this way, sir."

He nudged Jessica with his shoulder when she glanced at him, shook her head and rolled her eyes.

"Perks of the rich and famous, huh? The VIP lounge and then first to board the plane."

"Hey, you can always ride in coach if you'd prefer."

She pretended to be horrified and clung to his side, laughing. "No way! I'm already tasting my first glass of champagne. And besides, if I'm about to be poor as a church mouse, I might as well enjoy my one chance at luxury."

Nathan nodded to the attendant as she ushered them down the air bridge. *He was about to board a plane and head home.* Funny, but it felt as if he was leaving home rather than returning to it.

He slipped his arm from around Jessica and reached for her hand instead. She glanced across at him, her smile infectious. It was also hard to believe that this gorgeous woman was going to be in his life for such a short time, because it felt as if he'd known her his entire life. Letting her go was going to be one of the hardest things he ever did, especially now he finally felt like himself again. Or at least a version of himself.

Although facing his house, the office that he hadn't set foot in since he'd found his wife there, was going to be bloody hard, too.

"You okay?"

He squeezed her hand. "Fine. Just hard to get my head around going back, that's all."

Her smile was full of warmth when she shone it in his direction. "You could always stay. I happen to know of a little guesthouse that might like you to take up permanent residency."

They both laughed as they walked, but the truth was, Nathan was sorely tempted. "I'm just glad you're coming with me." *Even if it was just delaying the inevitable.* "My assistant's going to freak out when she sees you, though."

"Why?"

"Because Natalie micromanages every part of my life. Before I left there wasn't anything she didn't know about me."

They passed their tickets to the attendant and were ushered to their seats. The wide-eyed look on Jessica's face made him chuckle—he'd become so used to traveling first class that he'd forgotten how exciting it was the first time.

"You do realize you've ruined flying for me forever," Jessica said as she sat down in the large seat and stretched out. "The flight home's going to be tough."

He didn't say anything, because he knew he'd give himself away by smiling if he so much as looked at her—he'd already paid for her first-class return ticket, so she wasn't coming home coach class on his watch.

"So you and Natalie…" she started, taking the glass of champagne as it was passed to her by their flight attendant.

"We'll call for you if we need anything," Nathan said, nodding at the attendant after taking his champagne.

"Yes, Mr. Bell. Please do."

"This is insane." Jessica was sipping her champagne, surveying where they were sitting.

"Just don't drink too many glasses," he told her, settling down beside her and resting his hand over hers, knees bumping. "Otherwise you'll go to stand up and you'll be legless. It goes to your head a lot faster in the air."

"So back to you and Natalie?" she asked tentatively.

"Strictly professional," he said, before grimacing and changing his answer. "No, we're actually great friends, too, but professional in the sense that nothing would ever happen between us."

"So how long will we be flying?"

He shrugged and settled back, pleased that line of questioning was over. Natalie was his right hand woman, but she was with a great guy and he was happy for her. "Almost a day, including the stop over."

"Well I'm not complaining. This is amazing." She sighed. "We can watch movies, drink champagne and eat—"

"—pretty much anything we want," he interrupted. "She'll bring the menu over soon."

Jessica sat forward and leaned across him, eyes flitting over his before dropping to look at his mouth. Her grin was wicked.

"Or we could do this," she suggested, brushing her lips across his.

Nathan kept hold of his glass in one hand and reached for her with the other, stroking through her hair. "Oh yes, we can definitely do this," he murmured against her mouth.

He might be about to hit reality when their plane touched down, but for now he could distract himself with Jessica. And if he was completely honest with himself, his reasons for bringing her along for a couple of weeks had been completely selfish. He didn't want to deal with returning on his own when being with her took his mind off everything. Until he had to let her go, and then it would be hell all over again.

Jessica stood in the open door to Nathan's house and tried to stop her jaw from hitting the polished timber floor beneath her feet. Before they'd arrived she'd been exhausted, and now she was wide awake, looking around in awe.

"How was it you managed to put up with the cottage for so long?" she asked.

Nathan walked past her, flicking on lights and putting their bags down. "This place might look great, but your place has a soul," he said. "And besides, all the cottage was missing was a great coffee machine. Once she had that she was perfect."

Jessica kept moving through, taking in the white walls and the stainless steel kitchen, the huge pieces of contemporary art, the immaculately clean spaces full of what she was certain was designer furniture. It was amazing.

"Your house is gorgeous," she said. "Absolutely gorgeous."

"Wait till you see the bedroom," he growled in her ear, looping his arms around her from behind and kissing her cheek.

Jessica turned in his arms and let him kiss her. "So are we going to test the bed out now?"

She groaned as he pulled back, the last press of his lips to her cheek far too brief for her liking.

"I need to head into the office," he said, spinning her around so she was in his arms. His lips were soft to hers, warm and familiar, and she wanted them there all day. "But I'll be back in time to take you out for dinner, I promise."

"Sounds good," she replied, not about to be the kind of woman to moan about being left. Besides, what they had was only supposed to be a causal fling—it wasn't like they were in a relationship. "I'll explore this gorgeous house some more then catch up on some sleep while you're gone."

He grinned. "I know the minute I walk out that

door you'll be on the phone finding out when you can head out to see Teddy."

She tried not to smile back and failed miserably. "You got me."

"Go see him today," he said, "unless you'd rather sleep?"

Jessica shook her head. She'd love to go see Teddy, but...

He reached into a drawer and threw her a pair of keys. She caught them and looked from them to Nathan.

"Take my car, then you can drive yourself there and be back in time for dinner. It has GPS, so just jump in and go. It'll only take just over an hour if you really put your foot down."

Jessica pushed them into her pocket and put her arms around Nathan's neck, gazing up into his eyes.

"Thank you," she said. "For everything."

They stared at one another for what felt like forever, before Nathan kissed her and stepped back.

"I'm going to shower and change then head straight out," he said.

Jessica watched him walk away, eyes following his every move. She crossed the room into the kitchen and opened the fridge, surprised to find it fully stocked. No doubt his assistant could take credit for making the house ready. She took out a carton of juice, found a glass to pour it into, then leaned on the counter. There was no part of her that wasn't exhausted, but she did want to go see Teddy. She missed him like crazy, and she had a feeling he'd be fretting without her, no matter what the stable hand told her every time she called.

Nathan appeared what seemed like only a few minutes later, his hair still wet and dressed in a pair of suit pants and an open-neck shirt, gold cuff links glinting when he ran his fingers through his hair. His cologne wafted toward her, making her smile, and he raised his hand before he raced out the door. She could tell he was anxious to go, that he had other things on his mind, which was kind of strange because she'd never seen him like this. At home everything about him had been relaxed, whereas here he was the same person but different, focused on something other than...*her.*

"Have fun," he said.

"You too."

Jessica watched him go and fought the crazy feeling that the man she'd known these past couple of weeks had disappeared. It was one thing telling herself that they weren't in a real relationship, that it was only *for now,* but the thought of walking away from him soon was tough. She didn't want to rely on a man, to put all her trust in any man and have him turn around and hurt her. That was what her mom had done, and Jessica had ended up with a mother full of regrets and pining for the man who'd left her, and a childhood without a father. Her granddad had been all the father she'd needed, but it had still been tough, especially when she knew what her mom had had to give up to raise her. And she'd never stopped wondering what it would have been like if she'd had a dad, and her mom had had a husband.

Jessica rinsed out her glass and stretched out her back. Her mom was the reason she'd been able to ride and compete, because she'd sacrificed everything for her, and she was going to salvage her career and the farm in honor of her family—no matter how hard it was going to be to walk away from Nathan when the time came. In her heart she knew he was the kind of man she could fall in love with, if she let herself. *Only she wasn't going to.*

She kicked off her shoes, scooped them up and then collected her suitcase on her way to the bedroom, walking slow to enjoy the thickness of the carpet beneath her toes. He lived an amazing lifestyle here, but from the way he'd talked he could have easily left it all behind forever. Part of her had wondered if he might do exactly that, although now she'd seen his house and the type of life he was used to living, she knew it was a fantasy that would never happen. Which only made her all the more certain that she had to enjoy their time together, knowing that when she left, she was leaving him behind forever.

Tears threatened, brushing against her lashes, but she blinked them away. There was no use getting all sad now. She was about to go and see her horse, and Nathan had lived up to everything he'd ever promised her and more. Which meant she had everything to be grateful for and nothing whatsoever to be sad about.

Nathan closed the door behind him as quietly as he could, trying not to make a sound as he crossed the room and flicked on the light. The house was silent except for the faint hum of his refrigerator. He poured a glass of water, drank it down then headed for his bedroom, surprised to see the faint glow of a lamp spilling out into the hallway. He found Jessica asleep on his bed, wearing one of his sweaters that she must have found, curled up with a book still in her hand. Nathan carefully took the book and placed it on the bedside table, then pulled the duvet up to cover her.

He undressed and flicked the lamp off, bathing the room in blackness as he crawled in beside her. *Bloody hell.* He'd been back only one day and already he'd let Jessica down and left her waiting for him. After telling himself that he'd changed, promising that he wouldn't be the same man all over again, he was turning into that same guy he'd thought he'd left behind. It went against his nature not to throw every part of himself into his work, but if he did that again he'd end up in an early grave, alone in the world, or both.

He turned in bed to face Jessica, not touching her to make sure he didn't wake her, but letting his eyes adjust to the darkness so he could see her silhouette beside him. Telling himself he'd made her no promises about their future didn't help, because he didn't want her to go, didn't want to face the reality of her leaving for good. His problem was that his work took so much from him, and finding balance wasn't something he'd ever succeeded in achieving. He was either full on working or relaxing—neither seemed to go hand in hand with the other.

But while Jessica was here, he didn't want to disappoint her. That look on his wife's face still haunted him, the one he'd seen countless times but never so sad as the last morning he'd seen her. The disappointment shining from her eyes, the dullness in the way she looked at him—he didn't ever want to see that kind of look again, and especially not on Jessica's face. Not after she'd been the one to help him find his way back to being himself again.

Nathan shut his eyes, jet-lagged and tired from the papers he'd had to sift through. He could make it up to Jess in the morning—right now he needed to sleep.

His phone buzzed and he reached for it, checking his emails.

Or not. Because already Natalie had scheduled an eight a.m. meeting for him, which meant he'd have to be out the door before Jessica probably even woke.

Jessica woke to the crunch of paper beneath her cheek. It was the third time she'd woken like that in as many days. She groaned and pushed up, blinking in the bright light and squinting as she read the note. Nathan was beginning to make a habit of arriving once she'd fallen asleep and leaving before she was awake, and she was starting to get grumpy. She was about to flop back down again when she heard a noise. Jessica glanced at her watch and saw it wasn't even seven yet, which meant…she jumped out of bed, grabbing her robe and slipping it on as she ran down the hall.

"Nathan!"

The heavy footsteps stopped and she saw him, hand poised on the door handle, about to leave.

"Hey," he said, opening his arms as she walked into them.

Nathan dropped a kiss into her hair, rubbing a hand up and down her back. She inhaled his cologne, relaxed into his big body, cheek against the lapel of his jacket.

"You sure you don't want to come back to bed with me?" she murmured against him.

"Believe me, every time I leave you in there alone, it's torture."

"Then don't leave me," she said, pushing back to look up at him.

She could see the conflict in his gaze, knew he was being truthful, but she still wanted to make him feel at least a little bit guilty about going. She'd started to crave his touch, his company, and she wanted to see more of him.

"I wish I didn't have to, but…"

"It's okay." She pressed a kiss to his cheek, hands on his arms. "I get that you have to work. You've been away for months, it wasn't like you were ever going to be able to act like a tourist with me."

He looked away, over her head, then focused on her again, eyes locked on hers. The look on his face reminded her of the Nathan she'd fallen for on the farm. "You know what?"

She raised her eyebrows, waiting, still holding on to his arms.

"How long will it take you to get ready?"

"Ready for what?" she asked.

He grabbed her bottom, making her wriggle out of his way, laughing, all thoughts about being annoyed with him for leaving her long gone.

"Breakfast. Let's go grab something to eat before I head in to the office."

Jessica watched his face to make sure he wasn't kidding, and all she saw was a smile that told her he meant every word of it.

"Give me ten minutes."

He folded his arms and nodded, glancing at his watch. "Go."

"Just don't walk out that door," she said, moving backward. "You can't get my hopes up and then bail on me."

"I wouldn't think of it."

Jessica hurried back to the bedroom, grabbed some clothes and went into the bathroom. She felt as if she'd hardly seen Nathan since they'd arrived, and she needed a reminder that this whole thing between them wasn't something she'd somehow fabricated. Because right now she was starting to feel like a neglected mistress, and deep down she knew that Nathan cared about her as much as she cared about him. No matter what she tried to tell herself, no matter what she'd promised, there was no part of her that was okay with having less than a week left with the one man in her life who'd told her he couldn't commit to anything more than fun, yet somehow managed to make her care about him more than any other man she'd ever met.

So much for keeping her distance.

* * *

"I want you to know that I never meant to just leave you to your own devices."

She forked a piece of waffle covered in syrup before answering. "Is that the British way of telling me you're sorry for ignoring me all week?" The expression on Nathan's face made her reach for him, squeezing his hand and knowing she'd overstepped. "Sorry, that came out all wrong."

"No, it came out all right," he said with a loud sigh. "I'm a workaholic, and the minute I arrived back in this city I was sucked straight back into my old life. I tried to make it different and it just didn't happen."

"You never made me any promises, Nathan. It's okay."

He pushed his plate away. "No, but I was selfish asking you to join me and then spending every waking hour at the office."

"Is it worth it?" she asked, still eating her waffles and trying not to think about the first time they'd shared breakfast together on the porch of the cottage, wishing they were still there, that things could have been different.

He paused as he was about to take a sip of his coffee. "Financially? Yes." He shrugged. "But that doesn't mean that I shouldn't be spending more time with you instead. I just can't seem to find that balance, which sounds like a complete cop-out, I know."

"Nathan, I don't have long here, but…"

"I'm going to make it up to you," he said.

What she should have been doing was taking the

chance to distance herself from him, reminding herself why she didn't want to get close to Nathan, how much it would hurt to leave him, and instead…

"What do you have in mind?"

Instead she was lapping up his attention. Deep down she was lying to herself, hoping that somehow they didn't have only days or weeks left together. That he would stop spending all his time at work and turn back into the easygoing, relaxed guy she'd known when she'd first met him. That they would somehow find a way to be together.

"How about lunch?" he asked, checking his watch for what seemed like the hundredth time since they'd sat down.

"Today?" Jessica asked.

He frowned, reaching for his phone. He scrolled through quickly before looking up. "Tomorrow?"

Jessica smiled, but inside she felt like a flower wilting in the hot sunshine. Slowly dying but trying to stay bright. Lucky she was good at hiding her feelings—a childhood of trying to stay bright for her mom's sake, to keep her happy, was to thank for that.

"I might head out to see Teddy today," she said, even though seeing him again would only remind her that she was going to be heading home soon without him for the second time. That despite distracting herself with Nathan she was still on the brink of losing everything. "Tomorrow sounds great."

He opened his wallet and dropped his credit card on the table, then waved their waitress over. Nathan leaned across the table and kissed her, but unlike the usual spark she felt, the tingle that had run through her body every single time he'd kissed her in the past, this one was somehow tinged with...*sadness*. There was a finality to it that she wanted to stamp away, that made her want to kiss him until it disappeared, only she wasn't sure if there was anything she could do to take them back to what had been, when they were living in a little bubble outside of reality.

"Don't wait up," he said, slipping into his suit jacket. "You take the car and I'll take a cab."

Jessica watched him go and forced a smile when the waitress returned with Nathan's card. She was alone, just like she had been when her dad had left. Just like she had been when her mom had been killed, when she'd had to cope with the police arriving to tell her her mom hadn't made it. *Just like she'd been when her granddad had died.*

And she hated it.

CHAPTER EIGHT

"YOU MUST BE the famous Jessica."

Jessica turned around to find a beautiful brunette standing behind her, an earpiece in one air and a pen in her hand. "And you must be Natalie, aka assistant extraordinaire."

She shook the other woman's hand and smiled, knowing straightaway that she liked her. Nathan had talked a lot about the "other woman" in his life, and she knew from what he'd said that he'd spent more time with Natalie than virtually any other person in the past decade.

"I hope he's told you nice things about me," Natalie said.

Jessica frowned. "Well…"

Natalie looked anxious and Jessica quickly shook her head.

"I'm kidding! Honestly, he's told me that you're one of the most important people in his life. That he couldn't do what he does without you running things behind the scenes."

She looked relieved. "Honestly? Nathan is the

best employer I've ever had. He makes me work long hours, but he's done so much for me. I'd die if I thought he *didn't* say good things about me!"

Jessica was curious what she meant. Part of her had been worried that there might be more to their relationship since they were obviously so close, especially now she'd seen firsthand how beautiful Natalie was, but something told her there was more to the story. That there was nothing like that going on. It was her nature to expect the worst when it came to men—but she needed to let that go. Nathan wasn't her ex, and there was no other woman.

"Nathan said you've had a well-deserved break while he's been away?"

Natalie touched her arm and gestured for her to follow, holding up her hand for a moment as she answered a call and transferred it through to Nathan.

"I've had a seven-month vacation on full pay," she said, keeping her voice low as they talked and walked at the same time. "Not to mention the fact that when my husband walked out on me a few years back, Nathan paid my daughter's school fees and made sure I didn't lose my house." Natalie laughed. "And he paid for a terrific divorce lawyer, too, so my ex never even knew what was coming until it hit him."

Jessica was starting to get a picture of what Nathan was like in his usual world. He might blame himself for being a workaholic who didn't spend enough time with his wife, but he was generous to a fault in so many other ways. When he cared about someone he obviously had his heart in the right place, which was why he'd been so quick to offer to help her with Teddy and the farm. Maybe she shouldn't have gotten her back up and turned him down so fast—she'd been offended when all he was trying to do was help.

"So is it worth the long hours you have to work?" Jessica asked.

"Absolutely. I work hard, but I haven't had to miss one school sports day or prize giving. Nathan works himself to the bone, but he more than respects the fact that I have a daughter to look after."

It shouldn't have mattered to her so much—she was only here for a few weeks before heading home, which meant that what Nathan did wasn't really any of her business. But the fact that there was nothing going on between him and Natalie, and hearing how kind he was, did make her happy. It also told her that there was no chance of him ever leaving London for good, though, no matter how much she might have secretly fantasized about it. His work was too important to him. *But it was what she wanted, no matter how hard it was to convince herself sometimes.* She'd made her mind up years ago that she wasn't a relationship type of girl. She just had to convince herself that what she'd already had with Nathan was better than something long-term.

"So his office is through here?"

"Yes. Go on in. Do you take chocolate or cinnamon on your cappuccino?"

Jessica paused and looked back at Natalie. "How did you know I like a cappuccino?"

Natalie shrugged, the phone ringing at the same

time. "It's the little things that make me good at what I do. And besides, I don't have that many coffee orders to remember."

She watched Natalie go then knocked on Nathan's glass door, unable to see in without standing on tiptoe. There was a frosting across all the glass for privacy, meaning the office was no doubt full of light but Nathan and anyone else inside were kept away from prying eyes.

"Come in."

Jessica would have recognized Nathan's deep voice anywhere. She pushed the door open and stepped into his office, taking a moment to look around and survey the place where he spent all his working hours. There was a massive glass desk in the center of the room with a backdrop of the city below, two chairs placed in front of it. A modern sofa with chrome legs sat off to the side. It was more contemporary than she'd imagined, right down to the abstract artwork adorning the far wall, but then she wasn't sure what she'd expected. Maybe worn leather, a bottle of scotch and an old antique desk—like she'd seen in movies.

"Hey beautiful." Nathan dropped his pen and pushed some papers aside before standing and moving around his desk to greet her.

"Your office is gorgeous," she said, smiling up at him as he bent forward to kiss her.

His lips were warm, even more inviting because they were so familiar to her, and she sighed into his mouth. She could spend every hour of every day in his arms and never tire. When he finally pulled away

Nathan took her hand and led her to the sofa, dropping down onto it and waiting for her to do the same. "I had Natalie organize an office makeover while I was gone," he said, brushing her long hair back and over her shoulder. "She did a great job."

Jessica leaned back and crossed her legs, half-facing him. "Natalie's lovely. I had a chat with her before I came in."

A buzzing noise caught her attention. Nathan jumped up, reached for his iPhone and frowned as he stared at the screen. He started to tap away and she uncrossed her legs and leaned forward.

"Everything okay?"

He nodded but didn't look up. "Yeah. I just have a lot to…" He didn't finish his sentence, but reached around for his office phone and pressed a button. "Natalie, I need you to contact Leigh, tell him I'll have a revised portfolio to him by the end of the day."

Jessica stood, not sure whether she should stay put or leave and let Nathan get back to whatever he was working on. Instead she just fidgeted on the spot.

"I'm guessing we're going to have to reschedule lunch?" she asked, trying not to sound too disappointed. He had work to do, she got that, but she'd been looking forward to spending time with him.

"Oh, honey I'm sorry." He put his phone down and suddenly directed all of his attention toward her. "Is that okay?"

She nodded, planting a smile on her face. It wasn't as if she expected him to put his life on hold for her, but after spending so much time together it was hard seeing him like this, back in work mode and focused so completely on something else. And she hadn't even seen him before he'd left this morning.

"It's fine. I'll just…" She shrugged. "I don't know, but I'm sure I can find something else to occupy my time."

His phone started to vibrate again, and she could see how hard he found it to ignore the message or call that was coming through.

"Jess, I know we were going to stay home tonight, but I've been invited to a cocktail party. Tell me you'll come with me to make it bearable?"

"Sure." Except she had nothing even remotely suitable to wear in her suitcase. "I might have to ask Natalie where to go to find a dress." She also didn't have money to spend on clothes that she'd never wear again, not when she needed to save every penny she had to keep the farm going while she still could.

Nathan's smile could have melted her heart, but that warm fuzzy feeling started to fade when he pulled out his wallet from his pocket. "Take this," he said, slipping his credit card out and putting it in her hand. "Buy yourself whatever you want. New dress, shoes, beauty treatments, whatever. I'll have Natalie organize anything you need."

She closed her fingers around the card and looked up at Nathan, knowing that he genuinely thought he was just being generous to her and nothing else. To her, it made her feel like an expensive mistress, but that was only because she wasn't used to the kind of money he had. Nathan was just trying to do something nice, to pamper her, and it wasn't something she wanted to start a fight over. It was the same as him offering to help with Teddy, and she had to keep reminding herself of that.

"Thanks," she managed. "So I'll meet you at home later?"

He'd already turned away, phone back in his hand and a frown fixed on his face again. His eyebrows were drawn together, his full lips downturned in a way she'd never seen on him before. He glanced up to answer her, staring at her for a second like he was trying to remember her question.

"Ah, no. I'll have to stay here until later, so I'll send a car for you."

Jessica nodded and turned to go, feeling numb. She had no idea what was happening, what had changed between them, but all the spontaneity and fun they'd had, the closeness between them, seemed to be trickling away from them like a slow running current in a stream.

"Jessica," Nathan said, his hand suddenly on her arm.

She turned, feeling like an idiot for being so hard on him when she looked up into his eyes.

"I'm sorry about lunch. I'll make it up to you tonight, I promise."

Jessica pressed a kiss to his cheek. "See you tonight."

As she listened to him cross the room again as she left, she also heard him pick up his phone.

"Natalie, anything Jess wants, make it happen. Can you make sure she has what she needs?"

That sad feeling swept through her body again. When he'd said that in the past he'd been married to his job more than his wife, she'd wondered if he was exaggerating, that maybe his wife had been too precious for her own good. But now she was starting to see a pattern emerge that she would struggle with should she be in Nathan's life long-term. She'd probably end up speaking to his assistant more than the man himself, and anything they arranged would either be canceled at the last minute or rescheduled so they could go somewhere or meet with someone who was good for business. *Which meant she'd turn into his wife, into someone who resented the hours he spent away from home.*

And it shouldn't have bothered her, but the idea of going out and spending his money like some trophy wife just didn't seem right to her. A new dress, pretty shoes and an afternoon of being pampered was a dream come true…if she'd been paying for it herself.

Lucky she was only in this for the short term. *Or at least that was the lie she needed to sell herself, pretending that she'd rather be independent than dependent on anyone.* All her life she'd been a loner of sorts, when all she'd really wanted, deep down, was someone to care for her. Aside from her grandfather, no one had ever truly taken care of her, not ever.

Nathan ran a hand through his hair, leaning back in his chair and then spinning it around to look out at the city. When he'd been away, he hadn't missed anything about London. To start with, it had been unusual being in a different country, but he'd settled in as soon as he'd found the place he wanted to stay. Now that he was back, it was as if he'd never been gone. He didn't have as many clients to deal with, but he was busy with his other business and it was a struggle to keep on top of everything. Or maybe it was a struggle because he was trying to stick to more civilized work hours for Jessica's sake—and failing terribly.

He'd seen the look on her face today, the all-too-familiar cloud of disappointment and hurt that he'd seen countless times on his wife's face. Near the end, he'd thought his wife simply no longer cared, but now he knew that she'd just become an expert at hiding her feelings. Feelings he should have thought about instead of pretending that everything about his home life was okay.

He was at a crossroads, and he needed to figure out what the hell he was going to do to find some balance in his life. He couldn't punish himself with ninety-hour weeks again, but he also couldn't spend the rest of his life doing nothing.

A soft knock echoed on his office door, and he swung around to see Natalie standing there.

"I thought you were long gone," he said, rubbing his knuckles into his eyes and wishing he wasn't so tired.

Natalie's smile put him at ease, as it always did. He had no idea what he'd do without her.

"Ellie's with a babysitter, and Steve's going to meet me downstairs," she told him, holding up his bottle of

whisky and pouring small amounts into two glasses
when he nodded. "I'm going to get ready here."

It had been such a crazy day that he'd almost forgotten about the cocktail party. The last thing he
wanted was to network at a social function disguised
as a party, but it was the first time he'd been able to
accept an invitation in months. Plus it meant he could
spend the entire evening with Jessica by his side.

He took the glass she offered and finished the
whisky in two big gulps as Natalie took tiny sips of
hers.

"Did your dress arrive?" he asked, pulling at his
tie and discarding it before bending to take off his
shoes.

"For the hundredth time, you did *not* need to buy
me a dress or anything else for this evening."

He laughed. "Yeah, but if I hadn't you'd have had
to leave work early to get something from home. It
was a win-win situation." He inwardly cringed. Only
a short time ago he'd used the same terminology when
he'd been trying to convince Jessica to travel back to
London with him.

Natalie went to leave, glass still in hand, then
stopped. Nathan watched her, knowing she was waiting to tell him something, that she had something on
her mind.

"Can I ask what's happening between you and Jessica?" she asked. "I know it's none of my business,
but you seem so happy with her, happier than I've
ever seen you, and I don't—"

"What?" he asked, eyebrows raised. "You don't

want me to stuff up this relationship by giving all of myself to my work again?"

Her eyes were sadder than a puppy without its mother. "I love you, Nathan, you know that. I just want you to be happy, and she seems great."

Nathan forced a smile and watched Natalie leave. He wasn't angry with her for speaking her mind, because at the end of the day she'd just said what he'd been thinking anyway, and she was right. Jessica was the best thing that had happened to him in a long time, and he needed to figure out what he was going to do to somehow keep her in his life. They'd both agreed it was no strings attached, that they were just enjoying one another's company for however long they could, but he didn't want to let her go.

He took his tuxedo and white shirt from his office closet and got dressed, tying his bowtie and then reaching for his Tiffany cuff links. He would have preferred a night at home eating something great and with Jessica tucked by his side on the sofa, just the two of them. Instead he was going to have to wow her with a night out on the town, and try to convince her that they could make whatever it was between them work…*somehow.*

Jessica stepped from the car when the driver opened the door, a shiver running through her body when the frigid air hit her cheeks. Thank goodness she'd decided to buy the jacket the sales assistant had been so pushy about—without it she'd have frozen before reaching the entrance to Nathan's building.

She thanked the driver and hurried, moving as fast as she could without slipping on her four inch heels. It wasn't as if she was used to wearing such high shoes, and it was starting to snow as she walked.

"I think we might be heading to the same place."

Jessica clutched her purse tighter, trying to give just a quick glance at whomever it was who'd spoken to her. A man dressed in a black suit, bow tie and heavy overcoat ran a few steps ahead of her and held open the door—he didn't look like he was about to rob her, so she let go of the fierce hold she had. The warm blast of air from inside the building hit her the moment she stepped in, and her cheeks burned from the sudden, shocking change in temperature.

"Thank you," she said to him, as he moved through the door behind her. They walked side by side to the elevator.

"You must be with Nathan?"

She nodded, realizing who the man must be. "Yes. And I'm guessing you're with Natalie?"

He smiled. "They're the only two working this late, so it's not hard to guess, is it?"

Jessica let him select the correct floor, and they stood side by side in the elevator. He waited for her to step out.

"The best thing about these dos is they have plenty to drink," he said with a chuckle. "After a couple of bourbons the whole thing becomes kind of bearable. So if you want my advice, head straight for the bar."

She laughed with him. "It can't be that bad." If anything, she was looking forward to a night out, especially if it meant spending time with Nathan. "I'm Jessica, by the way."

He stopped for a moment and held out his hand, shaking hers when she offered it. "Steve. If you're dating Nathan, we might end up seeing a whole lot of each other."

She raised her eyebrows and was about to ask exactly what he meant, when he touched her back and they started walking again, across the thick carpet toward Nathan's desk.

"I don't know how many times Natalie has ended up staying late, traveling for work or attending things with Nathan. She's always telling me what a great employer he is, but they work long hours, and you kind of get used to being let down at the last minute." His grin made her smile, even though what he was saying wasn't what she wanted to hear. "All I'm saying is we could end up having dinner together a lot, because it would sure beat getting stood up."

Nathan appeared just as Steve finished talking. His eyes met hers before slowly traveling all the way down her body and up again. The way he smiled at her reminded her exactly why she was so attracted to him. The corner of his mouth kicked up into a smile as he stepped forward to greet her. If a man had ever looked sexy in a tux it was Nathan—the sharp lines of his black suit, the immaculately tied black tie, the white shirt against his tanned skin. The man was like a walking advertisement for a designer menswear store.

"You look amazing," he said as he took her hand

and kissed her cheek, his lips lingering long enough to make her melt. With Nathan, it was as if every kiss was their first, and that thrill of his mouth on her skin still lingered every single time. *Making her forget all her concerns all over again.*

She smoothed one hand down the satin-and-sequined fabric of her dress, still not sure she'd made the right decision with her purchase, even if Nathan did think she looked good.

"Did you have fun shopping?" he asked, taking her hand and rubbing his thumb across her skin. "I wasn't lying—you do look incredible."

"You don't look so bad yourself," she murmured, as he kissed the inside of her wrist.

"And I see you've met Steve," Nathan said, finally acknowledging there was someone else in the room.

Steve was now sitting in an oversize leather chair in the waiting area, flicking through a magazine, although he dropped it and looked up when Nathan spoke.

"Yes we—" Steve jumped up. "Hey, beautiful girl."

Jessica turned at the same time as Nathan did, to find a very glammed-up Natalie doing a twirl for her man.

"So who's going to be at the party tonight?" Jessica asked, as Nathan tucked an arm around her and they headed back toward the elevator. "A whole lot of stuffy old guys you need to network with?"

He made a face like he was horribly offended. "Are you calling me old and stuffy?"

Jessica pushed her shoulder into his as they walked. "Definitely not." She ran her fingers down his lapel while they waited for the elevator, pressing her body to his and tilting her head back for a kiss, refusing to think about anything other than just enjoying Nathan's company. "As long as you wear that tux I'd go anywhere with you."

He pressed his mouth so softly to hers he hardly had any of her red lipstick on his lips. "How about we skip the party?" he murmured. "Because that dress looks good, but it would look even better off."

"Always the charmer," she said with a laugh, slipping her hand under his jacket. His chest felt warm even through his shirt. All thoughts about doubting him or what she was doing with him vanished from her mind. He was an amazing man who had to work a lot—it didn't mean he wasn't the same person she'd first met. She needed to give him a break.

He groaned when she pressed a kiss to the underside of his jaw. "Maybe we could just stay for a little while, to make an appearance. Then I'm going to take you home and strip you down to—"

"Get a room, you two."

Jessica's face flushed at being caught out by Natalie and her partner, but Nathan hardly even blinked at Steve's comment.

"As soon as I've made an appearance and a few hefty donations to whatever charity they're raising money for, that's exactly what we'll be doing."

Jessica swatted at his shoulder, cheeks burning as she laughed along with the others. Maybe tonight wasn't going to be so bad, after all. So he'd brought her a beautiful outfit and paid for an indulgent afternoon of beauty treatments—he had a ton of money and he wanted to do something nice for her. She needed to loosen up and stop worrying so much. He had a demanding job, and she understood only too well what that was like—she'd put her career first all her life, too. Only now she was drifting without a purpose, no longer focused on achieving her own goals.

She reached for Nathan's hand and linked her fingers with his, looking up at him as he smiled down at her. If only they didn't live so far apart. Because this was the first time in her life that she'd ever met a man she could imagine a future with. And that was why her emotions were leaping all over the place—she was certain of it.

CHAPTER NINE

THE ROOM, FULL OF elegantly dressed people, was like nothing Jessica had ever seen before. Immaculately dressed waiters passed around food on shiny silver trays held high in the air, a string quartet played just loud enough not to hinder conversation, and all the women were dripping in expensive jewels. Add to that the posh English accents, and Jessica felt as if she'd walked into a party fit for royalty. She spotted a few younger women, but the crowd was a lot older than she'd expected.

"I'm taking it these are more your clients than your peers?" she asked as she stayed snug to Nathan's side.

His lips skimmed her cheek before he spoke directly into her ear.

"The older men are the ones investing money with me, hence the need to schmooze."

It was on the tip of her tongue to ask why he didn't solely focus on his other business instead of banking, when it was something that he could do without working such long hours or at the same level of stress, but she didn't. The last thing she wanted to do was argue with him when they were finally spending some time together. *She needed to let it go.*

"Once we've finished here I have something to tell you." His voice was still low, husky and just for her ears.

She tugged his hand, making him pause. "What is it?"

"It wouldn't be a surprise then, would it?"

His smirk made her place the hand he wasn't holding on her hip, giving him a cheeky glare, but before she could protest someone called his name and he turned away from her.

"Jess, come meet some of my clients," he said, grinning as he raised a hand at a group of men standing only a few feet away.

"How about I go find us some champagne first?" she suggested, spotting Natalie and Steve standing near the bar. "I'll be back in a moment."

Nathan gave her a quick smile but she could tell from the look on his face he was back in work mode. *So much for just the two of them.* No matter how much she tried to convince herself otherwise, Nathan simply had a different role to play here, and she needed to stop expecting him to change. This was his world, and she needed to suck it up and deal with it if she wanted to enjoy her time with him before she had to head home. *If she had a home to return to.*

Jessica pushed the thoughts aside. There was nothing she could do about that part of her life until she heard back from the investigator. At least she'd have something to focus on when she boarded the plane, because leaving Nathan was going to be one of the hardest things she ever did.

"Jessica," he said, his hand over her forearm making her pause instead of walking away.

"Yes?"

"It means a lot to me that you came tonight. I know I let you down today."

She shrugged, even though he was right. Half her problem was that she'd never been one to wait around for a guy or to rely on one, which made Nathan choosing work over spending time with her all the harder to deal with.

"We're together tonight," she said. "That's what counts."

He gave her another kiss, this time on her forehead, lips lingering for long enough to make her want to melt against him.

"I don't want to make the same mistakes again," he murmured. "You mean too much to me."

She let him kiss her, this time on the lips, before she finally made her way to the bar. When she glanced over her shoulder she saw Nathan patting a few other men on the back, laughing and joking as if he didn't have a care in the world. She smiled to herself. She'd had the very same thought the first day she'd met him, when he walked away from her across the farm. How incredibly wrong she'd been then.

Jessica sipped on her champagne, wishing she'd taken a few more of the blinis when they were being passed around. Her stomach was starting to growl.

"So did you have a nice afternoon?" Natalie asked as they stood side by side, surveying the room.

"It was lovely," she said, not wanting to sound ungrateful. "But to be honest, I'd have happily traded it for a few hours with Nathan." It was the truth and she doubted Natalie was going to judge her for being honest.

"Believe me, I know what you mean," Natalie said, her gaze warm. "And if it makes a difference, he's trying. He still beats himself up for what happened to Marie, and if he could change anything it would have been spending more hours with her."

Jessica was about to take a sip of her champagne but instead paused midair and held it down lower. "It must have been hard on him, losing her."

Natalie let out a big sigh. "Impossible. Especially when he blamed himself for what happened. I mean, the way he found her, the things they'd argued about the night before…"

A cold shiver shimmied like a trail of ice down Jessica's back. "I don't know what you're talking about."

Jessica smoothed her hands down her black dress, cringing as she connected with her bare thigh. She should never have worn something so short. It had seemed like a good idea at the time, but now she just wished she was back in her jeans, her hair pulled up in a ponytail and a tub of ice cream resting in her lap. Or better still, back home and riding a horse. And she sure as hell wished she wasn't standing in the corner of a crowded room, holding a glass of champagne she no longer wanted and feeling like an idiot making small talk with Nathan's assistant about a woman she hadn't even known. At one point she'd thought he was making his way over to her, but instead he'd stopped and talked to what seemed like every person in the room, and she'd left his side to get another drink and not returned. She was starting to wonder if he'd even noticed she was gone. And now she wasn't even sure what Natalie was saying, or trying to say to her.

"I guess I just thought, well, that after spending so much time with you that he would have..."

Natalie never finished her sentence and Jessica was left waiting, annoyed at what she didn't know. There was something weird going on, something that had been hidden from her, that Natalie was on the brink of telling her, and she wanted to know.

"He told me his wife's death was..." Jessica paused, trying to remember the exact word. "He said it was traumatic."

Jessica had imagined a car crash, the same way her mother had died, or a fast illness. But from the look on Natalie's face it was something that was hard for her to talk about.

"I hate that I'm the one to tell you, but it's not like it's a secret," Natalie said in a low voice, her eyes darting across the room. "If you stay much longer, it would be impossible for you to not find out."

Jessica looked in the same direction and saw Nathan, watched as he spoke to another man, his big frame standing out in the sea of black tuxedos and bow ties. Looking at him now, as at ease among this crowd as he had been mucking around with horses on her farm, she wasn't even sure she knew the man she'd started to fall for.

"Please," Jessica said, putting her glass down and staring at Natalie. "Just tell me or I'll walk over and ask him myself." She didn't want to be the fool, not in on something that Natalie had obviously expected her to know. *That she should have known.*

Natalie cleared her throat and raised her glass to her lips, before leaning in closer toward her even though there was no one near enough to hear them over the string quartet playing.

"Nathan's wife hanged herself in the office in his house," Natalie said, her voice barely louder than a whisper, her tone somber. "He arrived home late from work, on the night of their wedding anniversary, and there was nothing he could do."

Oh my god. Jessica closed her eyes for a beat and took a deep breath, her hands trembling as she tried to comprehend what she'd just been told. *His wife had committed suicide? How could he not have told her when they'd talked about everything? When they'd confessed so much to one another?*

"And everyone here tonight, except me, knows what happened?" Jessica asked, feeling as betrayed as she was sad. She'd thought they were so close, had shared everything about her own past with Nathan. *Everything.*

"One of the reasons he took off and went traveling was to get away from the media. It was front-page news that the art world's darling had taken her own life, and Nathan blamed himself for what happened. I think he still does in a lot of ways."

Had he lied about anything else to her or just omitted the truth about his wife? Betrayal stung her body, making her feel like such a fool. After vowing never to let a man lie to her, to hurt or betray her, now here she was finding out secondhand the truth about Nathan, just like her mom had found out about her cheating husband. Just like she'd found out the truth about her ex. It wasn't infidelity, but it was a lie that struck her right to the bone.

"Did he have a heart attack?" She needed to know that was at least true.

Natalie nodded. "He's always worked such long hours, and when she died he started to work around the clock without leaving the office at all. That's when he ended up in cardiac arrest and was rushed to the hospital. I thought I was never going to see him again."

Jessica picked her glass back up and took one long sip, then another. At least she knew now. Surely Nathan had known he wouldn't be able to keep something like that a secret from her. She could have heard it from anyone, read about it in the paper, even—and he'd just decided to keep it from her like she would never find out?

"I think I'll head home," Jessica said, trying to sound strong even though she was shattered inside. "Would you mind telling Nathan I've left?"

Natalie shook her head, eyes wide. "Jessica, please don't go. I didn't mean to upset you. If I'd even for

a minute thought he hadn't told you I would never
have—"

"I know," Jessica said, touching the other woman's arm before stepping away. "You were telling me
something that you thought I knew. That I should
have known. It's not your fault."

"But I've upset you." She grabbed Jessica's hand
and held tight. "I've never seen Nathan so happy, Jessica. Please don't go, not yet. Give him a chance to
explain himself to you."

Jessica fought the tears pricking her eyes and
braved a smile. She thought she'd been happy, too,
but the truth was that nothing had been the same
since Nathan had gone back to work, since he'd fallen
straight back into the lifestyle he'd told her so many
times he'd wanted to distance himself from. She could
only guess that he was addicted to what he did, to the
life he had here, to ever walk away for good, even if
he claimed that was what he wanted.

"I'm sorry," Natalie said.

"Me too," Jessica replied, her voice barely louder
than a whisper.

It was over. Deep down, she'd known there was
something pulling them apart, as if the bubble they'd
been tucked safe within back in New Zealand couldn't
keep them safe forever. She looked over at Nathan one
last time, before saying goodbye to Natalie, squaring
her shoulders and heading for the door. She'd collect her coat, find a cab, and let herself into Nathan's
place. If she was lucky, she'd be able to pack up and
leave before he was even home from the party.

* * *

Nathan stood still and scanned the room. She was gone. He'd looked everywhere for her, with the exception of the ladies' powder room, but no one had seen Jessica, and he was starting to worry. She wasn't exactly easy to miss in her short, black, sequin-and-satin cocktail dress, her long blond hair loose and tumbling down her back, especially amid a roomful of brunettes, and he was certain she wasn't in the room.

"Nathan."

He turned to find Natalie standing behind him. When she closed her hand over his forearm, her eyebrows drawn together, he knew he was in for bad news.

"Where's Jessica?" he asked, staring at her like he could compel an answer from her by glare alone.

"She's gone, Nathan. I'm so, so sorry."

He had no idea what had happened, why she'd left, but he did know that things had been strained between them the past few days. *Idiot.* He never should have come back, stepped back into the life he'd worked so hard to distance himself from since…

"You've got nothing to be sorry about," he told Natalie.

Her wide-eyed, guilty gaze said otherwise.

"It's my fault. I didn't know you'd kept Marie a secret from her," Natalie managed, her voice breaking like she was about to cry. "About how she died, what had happened."

Nathan groaned, but he wasn't about to blame his assistant. He should have told Jessica, had wanted to so many times, but after everything they'd discussed it had never seemed like the right time, and he'd left it wait too long. And now she'd gone, no doubt feeling like an idiot for being the only one not to know.

"Did she say where she was going?" he asked.

She shook her head. "No. But she was pretty upset."

He squeezed Natalie's hand and did his best to smile, even though he had absolutely nothing to be happy about. "Don't beat yourself up about this. Her not knowing was my mistake, not yours."

Nathan turned to go, but Natalie's grasp on his arm again stopped him.

"Don't lose her, Nathan. When you're with her, you're the happiest I've ever seen you."

He didn't answer her because he didn't know what to say. Natalie was right—when he was with Jessica everything fell into place. What had started out as something fun, a connection that was only supposed to be a holiday fling, had turned into something a whole lot more important.

Nathan stopped to collect his jacket and scarf and ran through the lobby, slowing only when he reached the pavement so he didn't slip on the ice. Snow was starting to fall, white flakes that would otherwise have been beautiful, but right now all he could think about was getting home. He needed to make things right with Jessica, because…

He jumped into a cab and gave the driver directions before leaning back in the leather seat, eyes shut as his fingertips started to defrost, painful heat spreading through his bones.

He loved her. Pure and simple. The reason she couldn't just jump on a plane and leave him was because he loved her. Which was why he was so embarrassed that he'd kept something so important from her.

His problem now was convincing her how he felt, and making her forgive him. He'd already lost one woman he loved, a wife who'd deserved so much more of him, and he wasn't going to make the same mistake twice. Meeting Jessica had been an amazing stroke of fate, but stopping her from walking out of his life wasn't something he was going to leave to the gods to decide.

"You having a good night?"

The cabdriver's question made him look up. He wasn't about to start sharing his life's worries with a stranger, so he just smiled and nodded.

"Good, thanks. Shame about the snow."

He also wasn't about to engage in small talk about the weather for the next twenty minutes, so he pulled out the paper folded in the pocket of the seat in front of him and pretended to read the front page.

Jessica swiped at the tears spilling down her cheeks, furious that she'd started crying. Her stupid emotions were getting the better of her, and she hated crying like some girls hated getting dirt beneath their fingernails. She'd fought the tears after her accident, refused to sob when she'd hugged her horse and left for the airport to go home, and now she was choking on tears that just would not stop. It was like a river flowing with no chance of slowing.

The sound of the front door opening and then being shut with a bang made her jump. *Please no.* She didn't want to see Nathan, had thought she'd be able to pack up her suitcase and leave for a hotel before he'd even left the party, but it seemed she'd underestimated him.

"Jessica!"

His deep, loud voice seemed to echo through the house, but she didn't answer him. Instead she leaned into the door for a second, eyes shut, breathing deep. She wiped under her eyes with the back of her fingers and patted her wet cheeks, opening her eyes only to look down at her dress. She'd kicked off her heels, but she was still wearing the satin-and-sequin number Nathan had bought for her.

"Jessica!"

This time she didn't have to answer, because he stepped into the room almost the moment her name left his lips. She folded her arms across her chest, the air around her seeming cool all of a sudden even though she knew it was warm.

"Jessica." He said her name softly this time, his eyes traveling from her to the almost full suitcase on his bed, then back to her again.

She had no idea what to say to him, where to even start, but at least what she was doing, or attempting to do, was obvious. Instead of talking, of looking at him, she crossed the room to take down the last things from the closet to fold in her bag.

"I know what Natalie told you," he said, standing as still as a statue. She could feel his eyes on her, knew he was watching her every move, but she still couldn't look at him.

"It shouldn't have been Natalie telling me," she managed, snatching her hand away when he reached for her. Then she stood away from him, anger replacing her tears.

"I'm sorry, Jess. You have to believe me."

She shook her head, fists clenched at her sides. "Your wife died in this house, the room down the hall," she said, "and you never thought to be honest with me when every other person in your life—every stranger, too, probably—knew what had happened?"

He dropped his gaze, shoulders slumping. She'd expected a fight, or anger when he saw her packing, but instead what she saw was defeat. Nathan knew how much he'd hurt her, and she hoped it hurt him like hell.

"You deserved better, Jess. I'm sorry."

"Sorry that I found out, or sorry that I ended up looking like such a bloody fool?"

He straightened and looked into her eyes, the defeated look replaced with something a whole lot stronger, more determined. She wanted to walk away, but she also wanted to slap him hard, to leave a red mark on his cheek that would sting and make him realize just how deeply he'd hurt her. But instead she dug her fingernails into her palms and stared back at him, refusing to look away. She might be angry with him, but she wanted him to know how strong she could be, even if she was crumbling on the inside.

Jessica didn't move when Nathan stepped forward, his hand reaching for her face, but she did flinch—she couldn't help it. She'd gone from craving his touch, loving his hands on any part of her body, to cringing at the thought of it. He'd betrayed her trust and she didn't want him so close, not now.

"I'm sorry because I love you, Jessica," he finally said, his hand falling to rest at his side. "I should have told you days ago, about Marie, and about how I feel about you, but I'm telling you now."

He loved her? Jessica took a deep, shaky breath and hugged her arms around herself. A few days ago, even this morning, those words would have meant so much to her, but now they just sent a fresh jolt of pain through her body, making the tears almost impossible to fight.

"Jess, say something," he said, holding out his hand and waiting for her to take it, the pain in his gaze reflecting hers.

She shook her head. "No," she managed. "How do I know you're not just saying that to stop me from leaving?"

His expression turned to anger—she could see the change in him. But when he spoke his voice was still calm, still even. "I know there's nothing I can say that will stop you if you want to go, but I'm not lying about how I feel."

She knew he was telling the truth, that he wouldn't, *couldn't,* lie about his feelings to her face. But she also didn't want to believe him, because walking away from the man already felt as if a knife had been thrust through her heart.

"Jess?"

"I just need some time to myself, Nathan," she murmured, turning away from him so he couldn't see the tears spill from her eyes and trickle down her cheeks.

"No," he said, his voice low before booming, *"no."*

She finished filling her suitcase even as she felt the change of energy in the room, could sense how furious he was. The next thing she knew, his hand had closed around her wrist and was holding her motionless.

"Let go of me," she whispered, wishing she wasn't so torn between wanting to hate him and wanting to throw herself into his arms so he could hold her and tell her again that he loved her.

"The weeks I've spent with you has been the best time of my life," he said, standing so close behind her, still with his fingers tucked around her wrist, breathing so hard that she could feel every exhale against her bare skin. "I tried to tell you, Jess, I did, but I just couldn't get the words out and then it seemed too late."

"Well you obviously didn't try hard enough," she snapped, hating the sound of her own voice.

The last few weeks had been amazing, but she needed to come to terms with what had happened, what she'd learned. And deep down she knew they were from different worlds, that if he had wanted to open up and be honest with her, he could have.

"I need some space," she said, refusing to turn back around. "Just let me go, Nathan. You need to let me go."

He slowly released her hand, and she sensed him step back, knew he wasn't standing so close to her anymore.

"I'll call a cab and have one waiting," he said.

She took a shaky breath. "Thank you."

Just when she'd thought he had gone, when she was ready to collapse onto the bed and sob, his deep voice echoed out.

"I was going to surprise you tonight, but…" He paused and she held her breath, waiting to hear what he was going to say. "Teddy's flight and quarantine have all been organized. He'll be back on the farm before the end of the month."

Jessica shut her eyes, fresh tears wetting her lashes for an entirely different reason this time. She turned, bravely facing him, pleased that he was standing in the hall instead of in the bedroom. *So this was what he'd been waiting to tell her.* With everything that had happened she'd forgotten all about the surprise he'd promised.

"Thank you." She'd told him not to do it when he'd offered weeks ago, but he'd gone ahead and done it anyway. She wanted to reprimand him, but the truth was that having Teddy home would be a dream come true, and she didn't want to argue anymore—she just wanted to go.

Nathan nodded, but before he turned to go she told him a lie, almost as much to convince him as herself. It was a barb that she wanted to sting when she told him, even though it hurt her just as much.

"It was only supposed to be a holiday fling. Just some fun, right?" It was what she'd told herself from the very beginning, even when she didn't truly believe it.

"It was *supposed* to have been, but you know and I know it turned into something a whole lot more than that."

He was right and they both knew it. The only difference was that he was ready to admit it and she wasn't.

Nathan stood silent and still in his kitchen, clutching the tumbler full of whisky that he'd just poured. He'd already downed one—his throat was still burning from drinking it in a single swallow—and he was almost ready to gulp the next when Jessica appeared. She was standing in the doorway, her suitcase at her side, her eyes red and puffy. Her usual spark was gone, replaced with a look that would haunt him forever, because once again he was responsible for making a woman he cared about deeply feel as if he didn't care one iota. And the reality couldn't have been further from the truth.

But there was nothing left to say. He'd told her how he felt, and now he was just waiting in case she changed her mind, in case she had something to tell him. What he'd done had hurt her, he knew that, and he should never have kept his feelings from her, especially not after she'd been so honest about why she'd never let men close. She'd been let down in the past and lied to by her father and a boyfriend, and that alone meant she deserved better. He'd known that, and still he'd hurt her.

Jessica walked across the room toward him, stopping at the table while he stood still at the kitchen counter. She glanced up at him, sadness like a veil over her face, and placed a key silently on the table.

It was over. He knew it was. And the worst part about it was that it was his own fault. Just as when his wife had died, he only had himself to blame.

"I'm sorry, Jess. I'm so, so sorry." His voice echoed out between them, seeming to boom off the walls. "If I could start over again I'd tell you, but I sure as hell wouldn't change what happened between us."

"Me neither," she murmured, folding her arms across her chest then seeming to change her mind and coming toward him.

She stood on tiptoe, painfully close to him as he stood with his fingers wrapped around the glass, trying not to squeeze it so hard that it smashed. When her lips touched his cheek, the soft press of her mouth against his skin, he shut his eyes, knowing it would be the last time she was this close to him. She was about to walk out of his life forever.

"Goodbye Nathan," she said in a low voice, walking backward then away from him as quickly as she'd come toward him.

He should have told her not to leave; he should

have told her one last time that he loved her; he should have done anything physically possible to stop her from walking out that door. Instead he stood as still and silent as a statue until he heard the bang of the front door.

Nathan shut his eyes against the fury building within him, threw back the double shot of whisky then hurled the glass across the room. His only relief was hearing it smash into a dozen pieces as it hit the wall and fell onto the floor.

Jessica was gone, and he only had his stupid self to blame. He shouldn't have been such a coward the day they'd gone to the market, because if he'd have told her then when he'd meant to, none of this would have happened.

He left the mess behind him and walked down the hall and into his office, staring at the place where he'd found Marie. It was a room he avoided like the plague these days, but the way he felt right now... he wanted to punish himself. Nathan dropped to his haunches, body suddenly fatigued, and then slumped to the ground with his back against the wall, head hanging between his knees.

It was then that the tears started to well, emotion catching in his throat so deep that it choked him. Everything he'd been through: the trauma of finding his wife, his heart attack, burying her...he'd never cried, until now. After everything, it was losing Jessica that tipped him over the edge, that pushed him to the brink.

A sob escaped from his mouth as the tears started

to fall and he surrendered to them, gave in to the over-whelming sensation that he'd lost absolutely every-thing he'd ever cared about.

Nathan sucked back a big lungful of air, trying to regulate his breathing and force the emotion away, focusing on replacing his despair with determination.

Jessica might need space, she might think this was over, that they couldn't ever go back in time and start over, but he disagreed. He'd spent his entire life never taking no for an answer, so why the hell should he walk away without a fight from someone he loved? Some people believed in letting someone go if you loved them, but not him. There was no way Jessica was flying away from him that easily.

He swiped the tears away and pushed himself up on his feet. All the money in the world couldn't make him happy if he wasn't with Jessica, and that meant he needed to face the facts about the life he was lead-ing. *Starting now.*

CHAPTER TEN

JESSICA RAN HER HAND down Teddy's neck and across his back. His coat was like silk, dapples shining through his dark bay coloring as he stood patiently in the sun for her to fuss over. She still couldn't believe he was back home, and she made a mental note to phone her friends back in the UK to thank them again for taking such good care of him.

But it wasn't just Teddy putting a smile on her face.

Jessica wished she could tell someone, that she had someone to share her news with. *Or a particular someone.* Not a day went past that she didn't miss Nathan like crazy, no matter how much she tried to forget about him, tried to hate him for the way things had ended between them. Because every time something happened, her first thought was telling him—she could imagine the broad smile on his handsome face when she told him her granddad's lawyer was going to be in court on fraud charges, and that she'd found a way to save her farm.

"I take it this is Teddy."

The deep, husky voice from behind jolted her from

her thoughts. *It couldn't be.* She waited for a beat, told herself she hadn't just imagined it and swung around to find Nathan staring back at her. *Nathan.*

"You do realize this is the second time you've surprised me like this." She should have been angry with him still, but after not seeing him for almost a month, there was a part of her that was just so pleased to have him standing so close again. Especially now that she'd had time to think everything through over and over, when she'd truly believed she'd never, ever see him again.

He took a step closer and the smile that slowly crossed his face was cautious. "You can tell me to get lost, Jess, but I'd prefer if you'd hear me out."

She sighed and shook her head. "You've flown halfway around the world to get here, Nathan. I'm not just going to tell you to get lost." Even if she'd wanted to, she couldn't.

Now his smile reached his eyes, that familiar eye crinkle telling her how happy her words had made him. When he was happy there was no way to avoid noticing it.

"Will you hear me out?"

"How about we go for a walk down to see your old friend?" she suggested. "I have a feeling he'll be pleased to see you." And she could do with the distraction of walking.

Nathan went to move closer then obviously thought better of it, shoving his hands into his pockets and walking alongside her.

"Jess, what happened the night you left..." He

didn't finish his sentence straightaway, but he did look at her. "I haven't stopped thinking about it since. We were so honest about everything else, and I never lied to you about how I felt. Nothing I ever said to you was a lie, and I need you to know that."

Ditto. She chose not to reply, because she'd said what she needed to say the night she'd left, and even though she'd missed him like hell, she didn't regret being honest. He'd hurt her, there was no getting around that, even if she was prepared to hear his side of the story this time around. To understand why he'd kept something so important from her.

"What I came here to say is that I was an idiot for not being honest with you, and I can only imagine how stupid you felt being my partner at that party yet being the only person in the room not to know what had happened."

"I just thought I meant more to you," she told him, pleased she'd had so much time to think through what she could say. The night she'd left him, the only emotions she'd been capable of were hurt, anger and humiliation—the feeling that their friendship had been built on lies when she'd thought they'd shared everything with one another. Now she wanted to understand.

"But that's the thing, Jess," Nathan said, taking a few long strides to walk ahead of her then blocking her path with his big body.

He stared down at her, not letting her look away for a second, as if his eyes were able to hold hers in place forever. She stared into eyes as dark as the richest chocolate and resolved to stay firm, to not just give in because she still cared for him so much.

"You mean more to me than any other human being ever has," Nathan told her, his eyes never leaving hers, never even blinking as he stared at her. "I love you, Jess. I wasn't just saying it that night. I meant every word, and if I have to spend the rest of my life proving it to you, then I'm prepared to do exactly that."

Her heart started to beat a little too fast as hope built within her.

"What are you saying?" she managed to whisper. He was standing in front of her, all the way from London, and surely he wouldn't have come this far if he didn't mean it.

Nathan lifted one hand and reached out for her, taking hold of her fingers and gently holding them against his. His touch made her tremble, sent licks of shivers down her spine. In the month they'd been apart, she'd gone to sleep at night and dreamed of Nathan's hands on her, of being in his arms again with his mouth against hers. And then she'd wake and be so angry with herself for the way she felt, but now… now Nathan was standing before her, and she wanted to hear him out.

"I'm saying that I want to be with you, Jess. I will do whatever it takes, because the only thing I do know about my life right now is that I want you in it."

She took a shaky breath to give herself a moment to think, to consider what she was about to say instead of responding with her first thought.

"We have completely different lives, Nathan. I can't move to London."

He smiled. "I don't expect you to. It's why I'm standing right here."

She almost choked on her words. "You want to move here? To New Zealand? What about your job, your home, your..." Jessica was sure she was dreaming. There was no other explanation for what she was hearing. *And she wasn't even sure what she wanted, if she could open up to him again and truly trust him.*

"There's a lot we need to talk about, but I'm standing here because I want to be with you, no matter what." Nathan's other hand cupped her face, fingers gently stroking her cheek. "There's nothing in this world I want more than you."

Jessica pushed into his touch, indulging in having him close again, unable to resist. "Why don't we go see Patch, and you can tell me everything," she said, prepared to hear him out. After everything they'd shared, what they'd been through, she wasn't going to say no to listening.

Nathan knew this was his last chance with Jessica— if he even had a chance at all—and he was going to say everything to her that he should have said before she'd left London. He'd never given up on a fight in the boardroom, and he wasn't going to give up on Jessica until there was no hope left.

"I really don't know why I didn't tell you about Marie," he said, as they slowly walked across the grass. "If I'm completely honest with myself, I've been ashamed from the day I found her, and I guess I just didn't want you—" he forced himself to get the words out "—to think less of me. We had this connection, and I was scared of losing it if you knew it was my fault that my wife had died. That she'd taken her own life."

Jessica made a noise that he couldn't decipher, and he wasn't sure what it meant. Then she reached for his hand as they wandered slowly, her fingers tangling with his.

"I wouldn't have judged you."

He knew she thought she was telling the truth, but he wasn't so sure. "It's easy to say that now, because you've had time to think about it. You know me now," he said. "But what if I'd told you that first day when you found me with Patch? Or that first night we had takeout?"

She let go of his hand and folded her arms, and when he glanced at her she looked uncomfortable.

"No matter what you did, or think you did, you can't blame yourself for her suicide." Jessica's voice was quiet but he was relieved that she didn't sound upset or angry. "Your wife took her own life, Nathan, and I can't imagine what that was like for you, but if you blame yourself for it you'll spend your entire life torturing yourself by trying to figure out what you should or shouldn't have done."

He braved a smile. "You kind of sound like my therapist. *And* your granddad, if I'm completely honest."

"She must have been a very wise woman, huh?"

Jessica replied with a chuckle. "And I know that everything Jock said was always worth listening to."

Nathan laughed. "I didn't think so at the time, but she was the one who suggested I leave my job and travel to some faraway country, and here I am. Then I met Jock, and then I met you." He looked into her eyes. "And you were better for me than any therapist, Jess. You're the one who made me heal, who made me whole again."

Jessica didn't reply. The smile that had been hovering over her mouth disappeared as fast as it had appeared. He knew he had to talk fast, needed to convince her that things had changed. Maybe she was surprised that he'd confided in her grandfather, but if she was he couldn't tell.

"Talking about my job," he said, moving to walk slightly closer to her so her shoulder was almost brushing against his arm, "I've been tying up some loose ends these last few weeks, and I'm officially retired. From banking, anyway."

She stopped walking and spun around to face him, her eyes wide. "You're what?"

He put one hand on her arm, stroking her shoulder then tracing his fingers down her bare skin. When she looked away he touched her chin and tilted her head up so her eyes met his. "When I lived here, I was a different man. It wasn't just you who liked that guy a whole lot more. I did, too."

"You did?" she asked. "You'd honestly rather be here than in a posh house in Mayfair?"

It might have sounded crazy, but that was exactly

what he wanted. "There's nowhere in the world I'd rather be than right here, Jess. I want to move on, and I don't want to be some jerk more interested in work and money than people."

"And how do I fit into this puzzle? Are you looking for my approval so you can move on with your life?"

Her question hurt—like a knife being jabbed into his heart. "I want to be here with you, Jess, here in New Zealand. I know it's a little country, but I'm sure there's plenty of investments to be made to make it worth my while."

He'd said it as a joke but he could tell from the crease between her brows that she wasn't sure.

"I'm kidding," he said, still cupping her cheek and rubbing his thumb gently across the lower part of her cheek. "I'm moving here because I want to be with you. In case I haven't made myself clear, I love you."

Her eyes were still fixed on his, but she hadn't said anything.

"Jess?"

"You know, all these weeks, since I arrived home, I've done everything within my power to forget you."

He baulked when she paused. "And?"

She sighed. "And I failed miserably."

Nathan tried not to smile. "So does that mean you'll give me a second chance?"

She shook her head and then threw her arms around his neck, engulfing him in a hug that was so out of the blue it almost sent him tumbling.

"It means I love you back," she mumbled against

his chest, face pressed to him as she held him tight. "I've tried so hard not to, but I love you so much."

Tears filled his eyes followed by a choke that he only just managed to swallow. He'd put everything on the line, risked walking away from the only life he'd ever really know in London to move halfway around the world to be with this woman in his arms, and it had all been worth it.

"So can I pay the cabdriver waiting in your driveway and bring my bags in?" he asked, his lips against her silky hair.

Jessica burst out laughing and stared up at him, her mouth wide open. "What? You're telling me some poor driver has been waiting all this time?"

He shrugged. "Hey, the exchange rate was pretty good for me, so it's only cost me half of what you're thinking."

She rolled her eyes and grabbed his hand before standing on tiptoe and pressing an impromptu kiss to his lips. Nathan wrapped a hand around her back, the other cupping her head, not letting her pull away. Instead he gently kissed her again, loving the soft moan Jessica made when he dipped her back slightly, teasing her tongue with his and stroking his fingers through her hair.

"I think you should go pay that driver," she murmured when he finally let her go.

"Oh yeah?" he whispered, his voice sounding gruffer than usual.

"Yeah," she said with a laugh. "Then you can grab your things and come inside."

"Really?" he said, grabbing her again with both hands and tugging her tight against him.

"Uh-huh."

He crushed her mouth to his this time, no longer content with being gentle when he'd fantasized about this moment for weeks—what it would be like if she heard him out and actually gave him a second chance.

"So no more guesthouse?" he asked, his lips less than an inch from hers as she breathed heavily against him.

Jessica shook her head. "I think you've made it to the master bedroom."

Nathan dropped a quick kiss to her forehead as she laughed, then jogged backward for a few steps before turning to run. "You don't have to tell me twice!"

He slowed to a walk, listened to the sound of Jessica's laughter and took a moment to look around, to just breathe in the fresh country air and appreciate how lucky he was to be alive. A year ago he'd just lost his wife and had a heart attack—there was no imagining how different his life could have turned out if fate hadn't intervened and let Jessica cross paths with him.

He owed a lot to her granddad, but he owed even more to her. And he was going to show her just how much every single day for the rest of his life if she'd let him. Because without her, he had no idea what kind of life he'd been facing right now.

Nathan whistled a tune as he walked past the house and out onto the driveway, pulling his wallet from his back pocket and nodding to the driver, who was leaning against the cab waiting for him.

"So what did she say?" the older man asked him.

Nathan grinned. "I'm bringing the bags in."

They both laughed, and Nathan passed him a wad of cash.

"That's too much," the driver told him, shaking his head.

"Then call this your lucky day," he said with a wink. "You listened to me talk all the way from the airport and you've waited here all this time. Just promise me you'll do something nice with your wife tonight. Take her for dinner."

The driver shook Nathan's hand and thanked him, but Nathan wasn't going to hang around to chat. He already had a mental picture of Jessica lying on her bed, and had no intention of keeping her waiting.

CHAPTER ELEVEN

JESSICA STRETCHED OUT one arm above her head, the other draped over Nathan's bare chest. So much had happened in the weeks since she'd seen him, and not once during that time had she thought that she'd ever be in the same room as him again, let alone in bed with him.

"I can't believe you're here," she said against his chest, her lips brushing the soft skin just below his collarbone as she lay on him.

He made a grunting noise that she guessed was a laugh. It sounded like a loud rumble. Nathan's fingertips were playing across her skin, stroking in long movements up and down her arm. The sensation sent tingles through her entire body.

"I've been wanting to call you," he said, dropping a kiss to her forehead and holding her even tighter. "But every time I picked up the phone, I'd start to dial your number and then realize I had no idea what to say."

"A lot has happened since I came back."

He went still, waiting for her to continue.

"I hope you weren't coming here expecting a damsel in distress."

He pushed her back slightly so he could look down at her and into her eyes. Jessica tried not to laugh at the confused look on his face.

"You're talking about the farm?"

She laughed. "I know you probably thought you'd have to write a big check to save my home, but I've spoken to the bank and everything's safe." Jessica had only finalized the details with her new bank manager the day before and was still buzzing from the news herself. "I'm not going to lose the farm."

"So you don't need my millions then?" He kept his face straight for a second before grinning, kissing the smile off her face before letting her continue.

"I don't need so much as a penny from you, I'll have you know," she told him. "In fact, I'll even be able to pay you back for bringing Teddy home."

He shook his head. "Not a chance. That was as much a gesture for your granddad as it was for you."

She sat up, bursting to tell him her news. "You were right about the lawyer," she said. "The investigator you hired uncovered everything, and I've already pressed charges. The serious fraud office is investigating his practice and the business manager's firm."

"That's great news."

Jessica was smiling so hard her cheeks were starting to hurt. "I've got a long battle to get any money out of him, but one thing Granddad did retain was a property in Australia."

Nathan's eyebrows were drawn together and she grabbed his hand, trying not to babble in her excitement.

"He owned a property there that his lawyer must have thought was worthless, out in the middle of nowhere in Western Australia, and I've already had an offer in the tens of millions. They've found iron ore there, and I'm selling out to the highest bidder."

"You're screwing with me," Nathan said, laughing as he spoke. "You've got to be."

Jessica shook her head, nearly bouncing on the spot like she would have as a little girl when she was hyped about something.

"You're serious. You're freaking serious?" Nathan's eyes were wide, shining bright.

"Tenders close next week, and suddenly my bank thinks I'm a pretty important client."

Nathan held his hands on either side of her face, and her long hair tangled around them as they kissed.

"You deserve this, Jess. I'm so proud of you for figuring it all out."

She kissed him again, closing her eyes and savoring the taste and smell of the man, looking into his dark brown eyes and letting herself imagine that she'd be waking up looking into those very same irises for so many mornings to come.

"I knew Granddad wasn't losing his marbles, but with everything stacked against him I was starting to doubt myself," she admitted. "And I couldn't have done it without you."

"I believed in him. And in you." Nathan said. "I knew it would all work out, but a windfall like that?" He blew out a low whistle. "Now that shows the old man was sharp as a tack."

Jessica didn't want to cry, but just talking about Jock after everything she'd been through lately upset her. "He would have loved us being together."

Nathan's lips making a warm trail across her forehead made her smile, his mouth then caressing the few stray tears that she hadn't been able to blink away as they trickled to her cheek.

"We've both lost a lot, Jess," Nathan said softly, "but we're strong together. I promise I won't keep any secrets from you, not ever again."

She tucked her body even closer to his, tiredness like an ache in her bones as she shut her eyes. Sleep hadn't come easy to her when she'd first come home. Then, with everything going on, she'd had so much on her mind that it had been almost impossible to avoid the insomnia that had plagued her. With Nathan beside her, she had a feeling that was all about to change.

"So what are you going to do? I mean, for work?" she asked as she listened to the steady beat of his heart.

He chuckled. "You're worried I'm using you for your millions now?"

She swatted playfully at him, laughing when he grabbed hold of her wrist.

"I just don't want you to be bored, that's all." It was true; a little voice in her head was telling her that this gorgeous, successful man couldn't be happy just pottering around a farm all day every day.

"I'm still the majority shareholder in the energy drink company, and I just signed off on a deal to expand into Australia and New Zealand." He held her wrist more gently now and pressed a kiss to the soft skin below her pulse. "I'll find the new sites, do the startup, actually get more involved in the grassroots part of the business. It'll be a challenge, but it'll be a change of pace. I'll be home cooking you dinner by five each night, I promise."

Jessica gave in again to her sleep-deprived eyes, listening to Nathan's voice and smiling at his words. "So you're going to be my househusband?"

This time his laugh was a loud rumble against her ear.

"You'll be training again soon, and a star needs someone at home looking after her, doesn't she?"

Her smile was even wider this time. "You really believe in me, don't you?"

"Yeah, it just so happens that I do," he murmured against her hair. "I'll do everything I can to help you get there, Jess, and I'll be with you every step of the way."

Jessica drifted into sleep, the sensation of being lost to her unconscious leaving her in a dreamy state. She could hear Nathan's heart, could feel every inhale and exhale of breath from his lungs, and the gentle touch of his fingers against her skin.

"I love you, sweetheart. I think I have from that very first night we sat and talked."

She managed a little nod. "Me too," she whispered.

Something cool touched her hand, sliding over her finger. The sensation jolted her awake, eyes popping open.

"What…"

She looked from her hand to Nathan's face, unable to believe what she was seeing. A massive diamond adorned her ring finger on her right hand, sparkling even in the low light. The small ones that made up the entire platinum band were equally as bright, twinkling back up at her.

"This," he said, raising her hand and inspecting the ring, "is my way of saying that I want to be with you forever. When you're ready to tell me the same, I'll put a bigger one on your left hand."

She almost burst out laughing then stopped herself, realizing he was serious.

"Bigger than this?" she asked. "I'm not sure that's even possible."

His smile told her that he wasn't kidding, and she was kind of terrified by his bank balance, but right now all she wanted was to lie in his arms and stare at her ring.

"Thank you," she managed to tell him.

"For the ring? You're welcome."

She stretched her arm out as far as she could above her head so she could gaze at it. "Not just for the ring. For coming back here, for loving me, for…" She paused and turned so she was facing him. "For everything."

Now it was tears shining in Nathan's eyes. "You're

worth anything and everything," he told her in a deep, gruff voice. "One day soon you'll realize I'm the lucky one and you'll feel completely duped."

She doubted it. "When you say anything…"

He pushed up on his elbow and looked down at her, bending slightly to kiss her mouth, lips barely touching hers. "Anything."

"I think you could start by making me waffles."

"Waffles?"

"Yes, waffles," she said, wriggling against him and moving her lips to his neck, teasing him with wet kisses along his most ticklish spot.

Nathan groaned and she moved back to his mouth, playfully nipping his lower lip between her teeth. He let her away with it for only a second before grabbing her around the waist and flipping her, making sure she was pinned beneath him, holding her wrists down so she couldn't move.

"You asked for it," he growled.

Jessica squealed as he nipped her lower lip, then her earlobe.

"Nathan!"

He laughed as he slowly released her wrists, his big frame still keeping her locked in place.

"Jumping on a plane and coming here was the best thing I've ever done," he said, suddenly serious as he stared down at her.

Jessica reached for him, cradling his head in her hands as she met his gaze. He was right—arriving on her doorstep was the best thing he could have done. She'd saved her property and her horses, and she had her man.

"The only thing that would make life more perfect right now would be a career back in the saddle," she admitted, stroking his cheek. "I just need to keep reminding myself how lucky I am that I can walk, right? I could easily have ended up a paraplegic the way I landed."

Nathan's cheeky smile made her push him back a little so she could study his face more carefully. He was up to something, she could tell.

"What? Why are you smiling like that?"

"I can't just smile at the woman I love?" he asked, far too innocently for her liking.

"That's your up-to-no-good smile," she said. "Tell me."

He chuckled. "Let's just say that I might have organized for London's best sports physiotherapist to take an extended vacation in New Zealand sometime soon."

"Nathan!" She couldn't believe it—or maybe she should where Nathan was concerned.

"Hey, I had to have something up my sleeve in case you wouldn't hear me out."

Jessica sighed as he lowered himself further down over her, hands on either side of her head supporting his heavy frame. She might never get used to the amount of money the man was prepared to spend, but she wasn't exactly going to say no to anything that could help her get back competing again.

"I don't know how I'm ever going to repay you. Or thank you enough," she muttered.

His kiss stopped her from saying another word, although Nathan did pull back for a second.

"Believe me, sweetheart, I'll think of something."

Oh, she bet he would. And funnily enough, she didn't mind one bit.

EPILOGUE

JESSICA GLANCED UP as the first raindrop fell on her bare arm. The clouds were starting to swirl, closing in fast, and the sky was turning from light gray to black. She sighed and nudged her horse on, out of the arena and back toward the stables. Their training session was over.

"You did well today," she praised, patting her horse and smiling at the way his ears pricked up at her voice. "Good boy."

"How did he do?"

Jessica looked up at the sound of Nathan's call and saw him standing just outside the barn, protected from the now big plops of rain and watching her. She stifled her laugh at how at home he seemed on the farm—his jeans were worn, his stock boots were scuffed and he was wearing a checked shirt with the sleeves rolled up, showing off his tanned forearms. Completely different to the corporate, Hugo Boss–suit-wearing man she'd glimpsed in London.

"He's amazing. You wouldn't believe how hard he was trying for me," she called back.

She halted her new mount when she reached Nathan, rolling her ankles when she took them out of the stirrups before swinging one leg over the saddle and landing with a soft thud.

Nathan's hands were on her waist the moment her boots hit the ground, and he spun her around to kiss her. She kept hold of the reins in one hand, and the other snaked around his neck.

"Ugh," Jessica moaned as the rain started to soak her T-shirt. She ran the short distance to the stables; her horse trotted alongside her and Nathan jogged with them.

"You looked great out there."

She grinned at him. "Great enough to qualify for the World Equestrian Games?"

His smile matched hers. "Absolutely. You'll get there."

Jessica finished taking the gear off her horse, gave him a quick brush then threw his cover on, aware that Nathan was leaning on the stable door and watching her every move.

"I still can't believe I'm so close," she confessed. "It wasn't so long ago that I was told I might not ever be able to ride, let alone try this."

"Jess, if anyone was ever going to do it, you were."

She touched her back more from habit than because she needed to, still half-expecting the dull throb of pain that had niggled her for so long. Even though she'd stayed so positive, she'd still wondered if it was a pipe dream to even think about making a career of riding again. And yet here she was, on an amazing new horse and already selected to try out for the top team. The team she'd known all her life she was born to be a part of.

Nathan reached for her hand when she walked out of the stable, a look on his face that she hadn't seen before, almost as if he was...*nervous*. Her thoughts flipped from riding to him, wondering what he was thinking, why he was looking at her like that.

"Why do you look like you're about to tell me bad news?"

She took a step closer to him, about to reach for him when an even stranger look crossed Nathan's face. Jessica stopped and planted her hands on her hips—he was definitely up to something.

"Take a look in your brush box."

She went from worried to nervous, her heart launching into a fast beat, pulse racing. Why did he want her to look in her brush box?

Nathan tried to keep a straight face and failed when Jessica moved her hands from her hips and folded them across her chest, fixing her gaze on him. Her expression made him burst out laughing—she expected some terrible practical joke to be played on her.

"I promise it's not a dead rat, if that's what you're worried about."

She pressed her lips together in a look he was certain was supposed to be angry but was sexy as hell to him. He'd seen her truly mad only a few times, and each time he'd struggled to take her seriously because of *that* look.

"Nathan," she demanded, "why are you looking at me like that?"

He shrugged, resisting the urge to kiss the pout from her mouth. Or, better still, he could have scooped her up and carried her over to the hay so he could tease her out of that look.

"Stop asking questions," he said, deciding to just stand still and watch her.

Jessica moved slowly and Nathan leaned against the door of the opposite stable as she bent to look. He'd expected her to find it as soon as she finished her ride, but instead she already had a brush perched on the door and she just used that on Sammy. His plan had been all about surprise, until she'd gone and changed her usual modus operandi. He'd watched her for days and never seen her bypass the box full of brushes and hoof picks when she brought her horse in after a ride.

"Oh my god." Her words were barely a whisper the first time. "Oh my god!"

The second time she was squealing, frightening the life out of her new horse as she spun around, eyes wide with excitement. She stood there, a little box in her hands, not moving.

"Nathan, I…" She looked from him to the blue Tiffany box in her hands, cupping it like he imagined she would a baby bird. "Is this what I think it is?"

He took a step forward and touched under her chin,

tilting her face up just enough so he could kiss her, stroking his fingers down her cheek.

"Open it," he said in a low voice.

Jessica swallowed, visibly, before tugging the thick white ribbon and letting it flutter to the ground. She looked up once before carefully taking the lid from the box.

"I'm getting it all dirty and it's so pretty." Her voice was so soft he hardly recognized it.

"We can get you another box." He didn't care at all about the box—what he wanted was to see her reaction to the surprise he had inside of it for her, and then the answer to his question.

As she opened the box, her mouth parting as her jaw dropped, Nathan lowered himself to one knee, reaching for one of her hands as he did so. Now he couldn't have wiped the smile from his mouth if he'd wanted to. He stared up at Jessica's beautiful face as she looked from him to the ring. It was a five-carat pink diamond surrounded by smaller diamonds, set on a platinum diamond band—he'd had Natalie help him choose it and arrange to have it sent over. From the way she was looking at it, they'd chosen right.

"When you said you'd buy me a bigger ring one day..." She laughed. "Nathan, you're crazy! This is insane. Amazing, but still insane."

He ignored her, not about to start discussing why he'd spent so much on a ring when he was waiting to ask her something a whole lot more important.

"Jessica, every day I spend with you is the best day of my life," he said, running his thumb over the back of her hand as he held it. "There's nothing I wouldn't do for you."

The tears shining in her eyes made it hard for him to continue. All he wanted to do was wipe them away and cradle her in his arms, even though he knew they were happy tears, but he needed to finish what he had to say. If everything went his way, he'd have a lifetime of holding her when she needed him.

"Jessica, will you do me the honor of becoming my wife?"

Instead of the yes he'd been hoping for, she gasped out what sounded like a sob, tears now falling freely down her cheeks. This time he did jump up to fold her in his arms, holding her until she pulled back and looked up at him, her tear-stained face brightening with a wide smile.

"Yes," she told him, arms looping around his neck. "Yes, I'll be your wife."

Nathan scooped her up into his arms and kissed her as if they had only moments together instead of a lifetime. He moved his lips slowly against hers, then with more intensity, smiling down at her when she put her hand to his chest and pushed back a little.

"Nathan," she whispered.

He kissed her again then gently put her to her feet.

"This ring, it's too much," she told him, letting him take the box from her when he reached for it.

"Nothing is too much for you, Jess. Don't you get that? I'll spend the rest of my life trying to prove that to you."

She shook her head like she disagreed, but her smile gave away her true thoughts.

"It's beautiful," she said. "Probably the most beautiful thing I've ever seen."

Nathan carefully slipped it over her finger, admiring the way it sparkled when she turned it toward the light.

"If I can't spend my money on you then it's not worth having."

The eyes that met his, the love in Jessica's gaze as she looked from him to the diamond then back again, told him that she was worth anything and everything.

"I love you, Nathan. I love you so much."

"Will you still love me if I tell you that I want a wedding with just the two of us? No fuss, no guests, just—" he paused to consider her face, relieved she didn't look disappointed "—us?"

"Just you and me," she murmured back as she stood on tiptoe to kiss him.

Nathan held her tight as they kissed, walking her backward until her back was against the stable. He was about to pin her arms above her head, show her exactly what he wanted to do to her now she was his fiancée, when a head appeared over the stable door, and her horse nudged them apart with his nose.

"Sammy!" Jessica laughed as she tried to push him away, but he only became more interested in what they were doing, nibbling the edge of Nathan's shirt.

Nathan looked down at Jessica and shrugged. "So maybe it'll be you, me and the horse."

They both laughed and gave Sammy some attention. Nathan scratched him behind the ear, and Jessica blew on his nose before tickling him. Nathan
might have to wait to have her all to himself, but he
wouldn't have had it any other way.

* * * * *

Mills & Boon® Hardback

October 2014

ROMANCE

An Heiress for His Empire	Lucy Monroe
His for a Price	Caitlin Crews
Commanded by the Sheikh	Kate Hewitt
The Valquez Bride	Melanie Milburne
The Uncompromising Italian	Cathy Williams
Prince Hafiz's Only Vice	Susanna Carr
A Deal Before the Altar	Rachael Thomas
Rival's Challenge	Abby Green
The Party Starts at Midnight	Lucy King
Your Bed or Mine?	Joss Wood
Turning the Good Girl Bad	Avril Tremayne
Breaking the Bro Code	Stefanie London
The Billionaire in Disguise	Soraya Lane
The Unexpected Honeymoon	Barbara Wallace
A Princess by Christmas	Jennifer Faye
His Reluctant Cinderella	Jessica Gilmore
One More Night with Her Desert Prince...	Jennifer Taylor
From Fling to Forever	Avril Tremayne

MEDICAL

It Started with No Strings...	Kate Hardy
Flirting with Dr Off-Limits	Robin Gianna
Dare She Date Again?	Amy Ruttan
The Surgeon's Christmas Wish	Annie O'Neil

Mills & Boon® Large Print

October 2014

ROMANCE

HISTORICAL

MEDICAL

Mills & Boon® Hardback

November 2014

ROMANCE

Mills & Boon® Large Print
November 2014

ROMANCE

ristakis's Rebellious Wife	Lynne Graham
No Man's Command	Melanie Milburne
rrying the Sheikh's Heir	Lynn Raye Harris
und by the Italian's Contract	Janette Kenny
nte's Unexpected Legacy	Catherine George
Deal with Demakis	Tara Pammi
e Ultimate Playboy	Maya Blake
r Irresistible Protector	Michelle Douglas
e Maverick Millionaire	Alison Roberts
e Return of the Rebel	Jennifer Faye
e Tycoon and the Wedding Planner	Kandy Shepherd

HISTORICAL

Lady of Notoriety	Diane Gaston
e Scarlet Gown	Sarah Mallory
fe in the Earl's Arms	Liz Tyner
trayed, Betrothed and Bedded	Juliet Landon
stle of the Wolf	Margaret Moore

MEDICAL

0 Harley Street: The Proud Italian	Alison Roberts
0 Harley Street: American Surgeon in London	Lynne Marshall
Mother's Secret	Scarlet Wilson
turn of Dr Maguire	Judy Campbell
ving His Little Miracle	Jennifer Taylor
atherdale's Shy Nurse	Abigail Gordon